secrets in the
house of delgado

secrets in the house of delgado

gloria d. miklowitz

Eerdmans Books for Young Readers
Grand Rapids, Michigan / Cambridge, U.K.

© 2001 Gloria D. Miklowitz

Published 2001 by
Eerdmans Books for Young Readers
an imprint of
Wm. B. Eerdmans Publishing Co.
255 Jefferson Ave. S.E., Grand Rapids, Michigan 49503 /
P.O. Box 163, Cambridge CB3 9PU U.K.

Printed in the United States of America

06 05 04 03 02 01   7 6 5 4 3 2 1

Library of Congress Cataloging-in-Publication Data

Miklowitz, Gloria D.
Secrets in the house of Delgado / written by Gloria Miklowitz.
p.   cm.
Summary: In Spain in 1492, fourteen-year-old Maria, a Catholic orphan,
becomes a servant to a wealthy family of Conversos, converted Jews,
at a time when the Jews are being expelled from the country and when
the Inquisition is diligently searching for religious heretics.
ISBN 0-8028-5206-8 (cloth : alk. paper) —
ISBN 0-8028-5210-6 (pbk. : alk. paper)
1. Jews—Spain—History—Expulsion, 1492—Juvenile fiction.
2. Marranos—Juvenile fiction.
3. Spain—History—Ferdinand and Isabella, 1479-1516—Juvenile fiction.
[1. Jews—Spain—History—Expulsion, 1492—Fiction.   2. Marranos—Fiction.
3. Spain—History—Ferdinand and Isabella, 1479-1516—Fiction.
4. Prejudices—Fiction.   5. Identity—Fiction.
6. Inquisition—Spain—Fiction.   7. Orphans—Fiction] I. Title.
PZ7.M593 Sd 2001
[Fic]—dc21

2001023893

www.eerdmans.com

contents

acknowledgments

I am grateful to a number of people who were helpful in the writing of this book:

Mrs. George Weissman (Mildred), who first piqued my interest in Conversos when we lunched at the Jewish Museum in New York.

Dr. Judith Laikin Elkin, a college friend and specialist in Latin American Jewish Studies, who gave me leads to understanding the history.

My son, Dr. Paul Miklowitz, who sent me a copy of Dr. David Gitlitz's immensely informative and readable book *Secrecy and Deceit,* about the Sephardic Jews in Spain during the period of the Inquisition. That book, plus much other reading, provided the setting and political background for my novel.

David Gitlitz, who so willingly read the manuscript for historical accuracy and who, despite his own busy career, responded to my e-mail questions instantly.

Tony Johnston, colleague, poet, and valued friend, who read the manuscript and never allowed me to doubt.

And my wonderful editor, Mary Hietbrink, who gave the manuscript as much attention editing it as I did writing it, always bringing intelligence and good humor to the experience.

aвout the story

In 1492 Spain was ruled by Queen Isabella of Castile and King Ferdinand of Aragon. Under their leadership, the country prospered. Devout Catholics, the King and Queen, with the support of the Church, declared Spain a Catholic nation.

First the Moors were driven out. Then the Jews — who had enriched the country for centuries with their contributions to literature, music, art, and the sciences. They were given four months in which to convert or leave Spain.

A hundred years before, under threat of death, many Jews *had* converted. They were called "Conversos," and as new Catholics could rise in professions to which they had been denied entry as Jews. But Conversos were never quite trusted. Some — though they regularly attended church — were suspected of secretly practicing the rituals of their old religion.

As this story opens, those of Jewish faith are leaving Spain by the thousands. Now not even the Conversos are safe. Inquisitors are appointed — monks — whose role it is to search out heretics, any who are not "pure" Catholics. Informers are encouraged to report transgressors. Once accused, the men and women are questioned and tortured. Many confess to anything to stop the pain. Punishment for the guilty ranges from fines, to life imprisonment, to burning at the stake in public ceremonies.

This is where *Secrets in the House of Delgado* begins — in this atmosphere of uncertainty and terror.

1

A WARNING

What should I do? Where should I go? Who can I turn to for help?

In the last days I have cried and thought and thought and cried. They are in heaven now, all those I loved. The sickness took them. Papa. Mama. My little brother Carlos, whom I buried last week. I am alone now and can no longer stay in the house where I was born. It is early spring and still cold. There is no food, no heat. No candles, even, and no money to buy them. It seems there is but one choice, one hope. The church. I do not like to beg, but that is where I must go and what I must do. Beg for help.

And what shall I do if I am turned away?

I hurry through the heavy rain, down the dirt streets of Cáceres to the Church of San Mateo, staying close to the walls and houses to avoid deep puddles. Few people are about, but from time to time a horseman trots by. His mount kicks up muddy water that splashes my skirt and cloak. My bare feet are stiff with cold, and I am wet through to the skin.

The church looms ahead. In the rain and mist it appears desolate and forbidding. I wrap my cloak tighter around me and hoist my small bag of belongings over one shoulder. Inside it will be dry, I think. I run up the last of the large steps, tug at the heavy door, and shake myself like a dog to release the wetness.

Inside the stone floor and walls give off dampness and cold so that it feels almost like outside. For a moment I stand still, shivering, hoping for the sense of peace and safety I have felt here in the past. The nave smells of candle wax and damp wool and human misery. In the dim light the old women who have come early bend their heads in prayer.

I slip into a pew, cross myself, and kneel to pray, seeking an answer to my hopelessness, but it does not come. Finally I leave the pew and slowly approach the confessional.

"Fra Adolfo," I begin, bowing my head and aching from the effort to restrain tears. "I am Maria Sanchez."

"Yes, I remember you," the priest says. "Speak, child."

I choke back a sob and hold my words until I can control my pain. "You knew my mother, but the sickness took her. My father before that. And Carlos, my little brother." I must swallow several times and take a deep breath before I can say more. "I am alone and afraid. I do not know where to turn."

Through the wood grating I can barely make out a shadow, and I picture the man who is that shadow — Fra Adolfo. His eyes are gray, like the stones of the church, neither kind nor cruel. His head is shaved at the top, but not at the sides, as is Dominican custom. His face often seems flushed, like one who is with fever, or who perhaps drinks too much.

"Tell me, my child, what I can do for you."

I close my eyes and clasp my hands tightly while I spin out the tapestry of my sorrows, the long year of sickness and death. It is a sad tale, and of no special originality, for many such as I have similar stories to tell. "Where shall I go? How shall I survive? Tell me what to do, Father," I finish in a whisper.

"Have you no other family?"

"No, sir. Only an uncle, Francisco, but I have not seen him in five years. He is a ship captain, always at sea."

Fra Adolfo does not answer for what seems a long time. I twist my wet skirt and stare at the wood grating, fearful that the priest will be angry with me for such self-pity. I sniff a sour scent and shudder at how I must look and smell, for my clothes are filthy, and I have not bathed in many days.

"You have known hard times, my child," Fra Adolfo says kindly. "I will pray for the souls of your family."

I cover my eyes with both hands and shake my head. Please, I beg silently, is that all? Just prayer? Help is what I need. Help me!

"Your father never came to church, but your mother was a good woman who brought you to us often."

A lump rises in my throat as I think of my dear mother and nod, though he cannot see me.

"How old are you, Maria Sanchez?"

"Fourteen," I whisper.

"Tell me, child, what skills have you?"

"Skills?"

"Can you cook, sew, clean, care for the sick?"

"Oh, yes!" I reply. "I can sew, though I am not a fine seamstress. I can cook, but only simple foods, for those are all we could afford. I cared for my mother and little brother, and can keep a house in order."

"Good. Then perhaps I can help."

Daring to hope, I lean forward. "I will do anything — anything!"

There is a sound, like a smacking of lips, a sound not entirely approving. Have I spoken too loud, with too much need?

"You may stay with the nuns for the night," he says. "They will provide you with a bath and clean garments. Tomorrow, after morning prayer, they will bring you to me, and we will speak again."

I press my hands against the grating between us. "Oh, thank you, Father. Thank you!"

"Tomorrow, then," he says, dismissing me. I hear him rise from his squeaky chair and leave the confessional.

The nuns are kind to me. In the morning, fresh from a good sleep and a cold bath, I dress in the rough brown smock they brought me and the leather sandals that pinch my toes.

After a breakfast of hot gruel, I return to the tiny cell where I slept. I sit on the wood chair next to the narrow bed and wait and pray — pray for my dear parents, for my beloved little brother.

"Come along, Maria," a sister says, entering the room. "Fra Adolfo is waiting."

The room I am taken to is near the sanctuary, a small office lined with books and almost filled by a large desk crowded with papers. The only light comes from a high window and a single candle. Fra Adolfo is writing at the desk. I stand before him, hands clasped, but he does not acknowledge me. At last he sets his pen down, blots his paper, and looks up.

"Did you sleep well, my child?"

"Yes, Fra Adolfo. Thank you."

"The sisters provided for your needs?"

I twist my fingers, not daring to look directly at him, and nod.

"I believe I have good news," he says, running two fingers along the sides of his nose.

I raise my eyes, a flame of hope flaring suddenly within me.

"There is a family here in Cáceres, the Delgados. They are Conversos. Do you know what that means?"

"Jews? Jews who converted?"

Fra Adolfo nods. "Conversos are new Christians. Some call them Marranos — swine." He smiles as if *Marranos* pleases him more. "There are those who converted out of true belief, but many took up our faith to save themselves from being driven out of the country."

"I do not like Jews," I say, thinking of what I have learned of them in church. "They do not believe in Jesus."

Fra Adolfo grunts approvingly. He leans toward me, his voice low and friendly. "The Conversos claim to be different from Jews, Maria. But many are not true Catholics. By converting, they gained benefits — positions they could not otherwise hold, acceptance in society. Those who pretend to be Catholics yet secretly practice their old ways — the Judaizers — must be severely punished."

I think of the last auto-da-fé that was held in the Plaza Mayor. It was a festive day with musicians and jugglers and many people who turned out to watch. Two Converso men were tried and convicted by the officials called Inquisitors, appointed to seek out false Christians. The men were tied to a stake. Then fagots were piled around them and set afire. I could not stay. The screams of pain, the cries for mercy upset me so that I nearly wretched. The smell of burning flesh hung in the air for days.

"Dr. Delgado is said to be a good Catholic," Fra Adolfo goes on. "It may be. He is respected and admired, and is physician to the Royal Court."

I glance for an instant at the window. Outside the great bells of the church are ringing.

"Dr. Delgado is away much of the time, and he wants his family to be well looked after. He has a wife, Elena, a beautiful and gracious woman who gives generously to our church," the priest says. "And two children. Juan Pablo, sixteen, is training to become a physician like his father. Angelica is eleven. A charming, engaging child much like her mother."

My mouth is dry. I watch Fra Adolfo's thin lips as he talks on and wonder what all this means for me.

"Now, Maria, I will come to the point. I have spoken to Dr. Delgado about you. He is very sympathetic to your plight and has offered to employ you." He smiles. "In exchange for food, a place to sleep, and a few maravedis in payment each month, you will be maid to their daughter, Angelica, and perform whatever tasks they ask of you."

I let out the breath I have been holding these last moments and shiver with relief. A roof over my head! Food to eat! *But they are Conversos — former Jews!* Still, I put on the smile that Fra Adolfo expects.

"You are pleased," Fra Adolfo says. "Good. God takes care of even the least of his children." He picks up a sheet of paper and reads aloud the directions to the Delgado home. It is in the upper part of the city, an area I have never seen. The rich live there and do not want the poor and beggars to loiter near.

"Go now," he says, waving a hand in dismissal. "God be with you."

"Thank you, Father," I say, backing toward the door. "I shall work hard to be worthy of your kindness and trust."

"A moment, child!" he calls out.

With one hand on the door latch I turn, wondering what more he will say.

"One thing I ask of you, Maria Sanchez. One thing of great importance." His voice is dark.

"Anything," I say.

"The Delgados are good Conversos, or so it seems. But I trust no Jew who converted. Many cling to their old faith like clams to their shells — often secretly. As they say, 'Many kiss the hands they would gladly see cut off.'"

My face must reveal doubt because he explains further.

"Perhaps they *are* truly Catholic. Perhaps. I do not say. But Dr. Delgado holds a position of great power. He has acquired much wealth. I question them all, even the good doctor. Does he pretend to be what he is not?" He runs his fingers along the sides of his nose and clears his throat.

I wait at the door, silent, not knowing how to answer.

"This is what I ask of you, Maria Sanchez. It is your duty as a good Catholic." His eyes fix on me as if they could see into my heart. "When you work in the house of Delgado, you must be alert. If you see anything amiss, any behavior that speaks of Judaizing, of the family practicing their former religion, you must come to me. Do you understand?"

I nod, so eager to be away I do not completely take in what he is asking.

"Go then," Fra Adolfo says. He bends his head again over his papers.

I close the door behind me, a squeal of joy almost bursting from my lips, legs dancing to be gone.

I reclaim my bag of belongings, say farewell to the sisters, and leave the church. Remembering Fra Adolfo's instructions, I climb the steep hill to the homes of the rich, to the Delgados, to my new life.

2

in the house of delgado

Thick white walls surround the Delgado home, hiding it from view. Yet through the iron entrance gates I glimpse the gracious house at the end of a long dirt road. Bathed in sunlight, it is huge, like a grand palace. Birds sing in the olive trees that line the road and conceal the building's entrance. And there are flowers — so many and such colors and scents! I grasp the iron gateposts and shut my eyes to remember their colors and savor their perfume.

It is another world. Full of light and beauty! If only little Carlos could have seen this place; it would have delighted him so. But I must not be carried away by beauty, I remind myself warily. I will be working for Conversos. Will I truly be a Catholic among other Catholics?

I set my small bag upon the ground, tug the bell cord, and wait, mouth dry with fear and misgiving. An old man in dark pants and a white shirt hobbles down the road to the gate.

"Yes?" he asks.

"Is this the house of Delgado?"

"It is."

"I am Maria Sanchez," I say, so softly that I clear my throat and say it again. "Fra Adolfo sent me. I am to see Dr. Delgado?"

The old man nods, selects a large key from a clutch of keys at his belt, and opens the gate. He waits for me to pass, then locks the gate and hobbles back up the road. I follow. He leads me to a side of the great house, through a door that opens to a kitchen where a cook is chopping vegetables and three plucked chickens hang from hooks. It is a big room, airy and clean, bigger by twice than the two rooms of my old home. Something savory is cooking in the pots on the large stove. My mouth waters and my stomach rumbles. I feel suddenly faint.

"Wait here," the old man says. "I will tell the Mistress."

The cook glances my way but does not speak. She is a small woman of middle years with a hump on her back. As she chops, I stand against the wall, eyes downcast, clutching the bag that holds all I own.

Presently the man returns and bids me follow him. I am thankful that I have sandals to wear, even though they crush my toes, for this is a grand house with marble floors and carpets as colorful as peacock feathers. My eyes swerve from side to side, glimpsing paintings in dark frames on white stucco walls, elegantly carved chests, archways and twisting pillars, large plants in ornately painted pots, a long table of dark wood that could seat a dozen people. I can hardly breathe, awed by such richness. This is the home of Conversos. I see nothing strange or different here, only finer things than I have ever seen before.

The servant leads me to a garden where a woman sits at a table, under a leafy tree, embroidering. She is a fine lady, dressed in silk and velvet. I have seen women like her riding in coaches to church on Sunday. Her eyes are dark and almond shaped, and the skin of her round face is soft and unlined. I look away when I think of my mother's tired eyes and pinched face and how she dragged herself about even to the day she died. The lady examines me with a kindly look while I tremble. She nods to the servant, who moves off a short distance, turns his back, and waits.

"Do not be afraid, child," the lady says. "Look at me."

I raise my eyes and bite my lip to control the shivering.

"Are you hungry?"

"No, lady," I lie. "The nuns gave me breakfast."

"You are Maria Sanchez?"

"Yes, lady."

"I am Doña Elena Delgado." She smiles.

I take a deep breath and try to return her smile, but

I am too frightened and confused. Will the Mistress like me enough to let me stay?

"Welcome to my home, Maria. *Your* home, too, now. You will be treated fairly here. You will have food, shelter, clothing — and a few maravedis each month to spend as you wish. In return we expect honesty, hard work, and loyalty."

I gasp, awed by her generosity and kindness, which seem genuine.

"Your primary duty will be to serve my daughter, Angelica." Doña Elena's eyes sparkle as if just saying her daughter's name gives her pleasure. "She is a willful child. Not always obedient, and sometimes lacking in judgment in matters that might endanger her. Nevertheless . . . these are the very characteristics that make her endearing." She pauses and thinks a moment. "I will expect you to care for Angelica's needs and protect her from her wilder whims. In addition, you will be called upon to help the other staff as time permits. I assume that is suitable?"

"Oh, yes!" I nearly sing.

"Good." She takes up her embroidery again and says, "That will be all, then. Roberto?"

The old man returns to us. "Take Maria to Margarita."

I curtsy and thank Doña Elena, then follow Roberto out of the garden back into the house.

It is a wonder, this place. Servants are polishing silver in one room. In another, flowers are being cut and arranged in ceramic vases. From a distant room I hear music and laughter. For an instant I shiver as Fra Adolfo's orders come to mind, but I will not let his words blunt my growing joy. This seems a good place with good people. A place to work that would have made my mother happy for me. I will do everything I can to make the Delgados glad they have taken me in.

3

I meet the family

Roberto gives me over to Margarita, the housekeeper, and goes his way. She is a plump woman with gray hair gathered in a large knot at the back of her head.

"Poor child," she says, regarding me kindly. "The Mistress has told me about your misfortunes. Such terrible times these are. I myself lost a child to the sickness and a husband to the bandits on the road." Her voice nearly breaks, but she recovers quickly. "You will like it here. There are no better people to work for than the Delgados. They treat us like family.

"Come. I will show you your room, and then bring you to meet the young mistress, Angelica."

"I hope she will like me," I say softly.

"Angelica?" She chuckles. "She is a lively one, that child, sometimes a handful of trouble — not at all like her name. But do not fear. She will like you, and you her. I know."

On the way to my room in a wing of the house near the kitchen, Margarita introduces me to the other servants. There is Roberto, who, because of his age, divides his time between the house and the stables. And there is Luis, the man I saw earlier polishing silver in the dining room, Vera the cook, and four others. Everyone greets me warmly.

My room is simple and bright, much nicer than the dark room I shared with Mama, Papa, and my little brother. Against one wall are two narrow beds with a small stand between them. Jesus looks down from a painting above one of the beds. Margarita tells me that the bed belongs to Serena, another servant, and that I am to share the room with her. "A good girl not much older than you," she says, "though a little slow in the head." Across from the beds is a wooden chest of drawers. On top are a pitcher and basin for washing, two candlesticks, and a brush and comb. I hang my cloak on a hook near the door next to a slop pail on the wooden floor.

Margarita leans against the door frame, watching as I store my few belongings. For a long moment I pause, uncertain of where to put the charcoal drawing that I made of Mama and Carlos a year ago. Though slightly smudged, it stirs memories that flood my chest with pain. Finally I lay it on the stand between the beds.

"Your family?" Margarita asks.

"My mother and brother."

She comes closer, picks up the drawing, and examines it. "Who drew this?"

"I did."

"You have talent."

Heat rises to my face. I have been drawing with clumps of fireplace charcoal since I was small, but no one, not even my mother, ever called me talented. "Thank you," I say in a small voice.

"Come, Maria," Margarita says when I am ready. "We will find Angelica. She is taking her music lesson now."

She leads the way through the house to a room off a large salon. The music I heard when I first entered the house comes from a boxlike instrument on legs, with white and black keys. Margarita says that it is a harpsichord and that few people are fortunate enough to own one.

A slender man wearing black breeches and a white shirt with billowing sleeves stands with his back to us. Seated on a bench playing the harpsichord is a young girl.

"Shame on you, Angelica!" the music master roars. "That is abominable! What good are lessons if you do not practice? You waste my time and your parents' money. Your mother will learn of this!"

"No!" The girl pounds the keys with both hands so the harpsichord blasts out a terrible sound. I clap my hands over my ears, and Margarita raises her eyes to heaven and sighs. As the awful noise fades, Angelica sweetly asks, "Is that better, Maestro Suarez?"

"Sister! Behave yourself!" a male voice calls from the other end of the room. A young man strides forward. He must be the brother Fra Adolfo mentioned. Dressed in riding clothes and boots, he is tall, with fair skin, dark eyes, and thick, shiny black hair. He is so handsome I feel a rush of heat through me and press a finger over my lips to still the sound that would burst forth.

"Juan Pablo," Margarita whispers, as we stand in the doorway. "A fine young master, he is. Someday he will be a physician like his father."

Angelica pounds the poor instrument again and cries, "I *will not* behave! Practice is so *boring!* I want to be outdoors playing with the cat! I want to be free like the town children! I want . . ."

"Enough!" Juan Pablo commands, touching his sister's curly head in a way that softens his firm tone. "Please excuse Angelica's bad manners, Maestro Suarez," he says to the music master. "I will see that she is better prepared for your lesson next week. Thank you, Maestro, and good day."

The music master appears relieved. He bows slightly and leaves the room, passing Margarita and me. It is then that Juan Pablo notices us.

"Yes?" he asks, one hand on his sister's shoulder. "Is there something you want, Margarita?"

"Yes, young master. Your mother has engaged a

new servant to care for Angelica. She asked me to introduce her."

"Come forward," he says.

Angelica, still on the music bench, swings around to inspect us. She is a pretty child with a head of reddish-brown curls and olive skin with a rosy tint. Her eyes twinkle as she looks me over. But my eyes stray to her brother.

Margarita places an arm around my shoulder. "Angelica, this is Maria Sanchez. She will be your mistress-in-waiting."

"Good," Juan Pablo says. "I told Mother that Angelica needs someone to keep her from mischief."

Angelica giggles. I think she is flattered by her brother's words but certain that no one will keep her from doing what she wishes. She tilts her head, appraising me as if I am a piece of furniture, and says, "She is pretty, but that gown — it is hideous!"

I bow my head. The dress the nuns gave me is the best I have.

"Angelica!" Juan Pablo exclaims, then addresses me. "My sister has yet to learn manners. Forgive her." He extends a hand. "I am Juan Pablo Delgado."

The hand I give him is cold and damp, and my face burns at his touch.

Angelica crosses her arms over her thin chest and proclaims, "She likes you, brother. See how she blushes! Look at her eyes! Am I right, Maria?"

I am so embarrassed that I can find no words to reply. Juan Pablo must think that I am dumb, for I can only stare at the floor, tongue-tied.

"And *I* like her," he says, smoothing over my awkwardness. "And you will too, dear sister, as you get to know her." He turns to me. "I hope you will be happy here, Maria Sanchez. But beware. My sister is a charming little devil. She is irreverent, wild, and used to having her own way. Still, I believe she is good at heart." He smiles at Angelica. "And now I must go."

Angelica sticks out her tongue at her brother's retreating back. I bite my lip so as not to laugh. She jumps off the music bench, throws her arms around my waist, and exclaims, "I am so glad you are here! I am sorry if I embarrassed you, Maria. Sometimes I say things without thinking. We are going to be great friends. I just know it!" She turns to Margarita. "You may go now. I will show Maria all she needs to know."

"Come." She takes my hand with such instant trust that I feel more like a child than her guardian. "First, we must find you some proper clothes." She puts a finger to her lips in a thoughtful pose, then skips ahead of me and looks back. "I do not want my mistress-in-waiting to look like a mouse. No. You must wear colors *I* like! Yes! I shall get Mama to order a dress for you to wear to church — in bright blue, to set off your dark hair — and another for everyday. Gray-green, I think, because your eyes are that color. Is there anything you need? Shoes — of course. A hairbrush? Books to read when you are done with your work?"

"I cannot read, young mistress," I say.

"Of course! I should have thought. But — no matter. I shall teach you."

"But . . . !" I am shocked. In this country girls are not taught to read, certainly not those from poor families. Perhaps in families of great means those rules do not apply. When I show my alarm, Angelica holds up a hand.

"Do not deny me! I shall teach you whether or not it is proper. It will be our special secret."

One moment Angelica is thoughtless and irreverent, the next caring and thoughtful. I am confused by how quickly she changes.

She leads me up the broad carpeted stairway to her room above the main salon, explaining, as we go, who sleeps behind each door. Her room overlooks the garden, and when she flings open a wooden shutter to let in air and light, the sweet scent of jasmine fills the room.

"These are my clothes," Angelica says, opening a large carved wardrobe to show me dresses and cloaks in every color, of the finest silks and velvets. I am overwhelmed by the brilliant array. "And these — my shoes. Each day I will tell you what it is I wish to wear, and you will help me dress." Her eyes shine with a devilish gleam. "I do not need such help, of course," she confesses. "I am eleven years old and perfectly able to dress myself."

Then what is my purpose, I wonder, listening but saying nothing.

Angelica drops down on her large four-poster bed with its thick, embroidered comforter and folds her hands. "Mama and Papa think I need someone to watch over me. Let them think so if that is what brings you here. My parents have few friends. None have children my age. I long for a friend, Maria, not a guard for my safety or someone to report what I do to my parents. I long for someone to play with and talk to. Will you be my friend, Maria?"

I miss my beloved family. I am in a strange home. I do not really know these people. They may even be Judaizers, though I see no sign of that.

How do I answer Angelica?

4

angelica's gift

"I have a surprise for you," Angelica says one day soon after my arrival.

She bubbles with suppressed delight and tries to hide it.

It is three weeks before Easter. I close the book she has been teaching me to read and stretch to loosen the stiffness in my neck. I am a bit uneasy when Angelica has a "surprise." Last week, for instance, we entered Dr. Delgado's library, a room forbidden to her. She removed a book she had no permission to take.

"Come with me," she says, grabbing my hand and pulling me along. "To Mama's room."

I never go into Doña Elena's room. It is Margarita's job to care for the Mistress and her things, so I am especially curious.

"Mama?" Angelica calls, knocking on the door. "We are here."

"Yes — come in, dear," Doña Elena calls back. When we enter, she smiles at us from a small desk near a window. It is a bright, spacious room with a silver cross on the wall above a four-poster bed. On each side of the bed are beautifully carved wooden chests, which face a wardrobe even bigger than the one in Angelica's room. There are paintings on each wall. Flowers as cheerful as spring spill from vases. The upholstered chairs and lush bed coverings are shades of green and yellow, like spring itself.

I have hardly spoken with the Mistress since I came and cannot imagine why I am here.

"Maria, dear," Doña Elena says after our greetings. "Easter is coming, and we thought you might like this. Angelica . . ." She nods to a package on a table near the bed, and Angelica brings it to me.

"This is the surprise, Maria. I chose it myself. I hope you like it," she says.

"But . . . what. . . ." My face burns at this special attention, and I bite my lip to stop the happy tears.

"Sit down, dear, and open it," Doña Elena says, motioning to a chair nearby.

I sit and stare at the wrapping, then slowly undo it, taking care to smooth the paper so it may be used again.

Inside is a garment — blue, of a soft woolen fabric. I let out the breath I was holding and look up at Angelica and her mother.

"Let us see it! For heaven's sake, Maria, hold it up!" Angelica cries, impatient with me.

I lift the garment carefully, stand, and hold it so that its length falls in front of me. It is a dress with white lace trim around the neck. The color is as deep blue as the sky just before morning. I open my mouth to speak but cannot. At last, my voice husky, I ask, "For me?"

"Of course, silly," Angelica giggles. "I told you when you first came that you must have a fine dress for church and others for everyday. Try it on. Come. Mother's dressing room has a good mirror."

"It is lovely on you, Maria," Doña Elena says when I come back to show myself. "Turn around."

I twirl about, smoothing the soft wool against my hips, smiling. If only Mama could see me now! I feel different — not like a servant, but like a lady, a princess. I laugh with joy. It is beautiful, and much too fine for such as me.

"I told you, Mama — I told you she would love it. Blue is her best color! Now she must fix her hair and wear proper shoes. . . ." Angelica puts a finger to her lips as she assesses me. "Take off your cap, Maria, and let your hair down."

When I do as she asks, she beams. "Yes! Oh, yes! Mama? Can she come to church with us on Good Friday or Easter Sunday?"

Doña Elena's eyes widen, and her face loses its color. It feels like the air has suddenly drained from the room. "That is a question for later, Angelica." The Mistress picks up her pen and turns back to her writing. "Away with you two, now. I have things to do."

"Mama?"

"Come, Angelica," I say. "We must go. And thank you, Mistress. Thank you for your kindness. I have never had so fine a present." In awkward silence I hurriedly gather up the gift wrappings and my old dress and leave the room with Angelica in tow.

The two of us part in the hallway — she to go for her music lesson, I to change back to my regular dress and put away my gift. She insists she will speak again with Doña Elena about Easter, though I beg her not to. Still, I dare to hope that I may join them on one of the special days.

It is strange to walk the halls dressed so fine, with my hair loose around my shoulders as it is when I go to sleep at night. I feel flushed and unreal, as if I am floating in a dream, when Juan Pablo begins climbing the stairs just as I start down.

"Oh!" I exclaim, stopping and pressing a hand to my mouth.

"Maria?" he asks, as if not quite sure.

I nod.

"You look . . ." He does not finish, but his admiring glance lingers on me.

"I am sorry . . . " I start to babble and feel a self-conscious smile start at my lips. "Your mother and sister gave me this . . . gown and had me put it on . . . so they could see. . . . I am just going to my room to change."

"No need to explain, Maria. I was just surprised! You look — beautiful."

I cannot take my eyes from his. "Gracias," I whisper. "Con permisso. . . ." I sweep past him down the stairs, my heart hammering in my chest. When I reach the bottom step, I glance back. Juan Pablo has not moved. He smiles down at me, bows, then bounds up the stairs.

In the next weeks Angelica and I share the days and come to know each other better. Together we explore every nook and cranny of the big house and grounds. She reveals secret places where she can listen to the servants talk, where she can hear what her father says when visitors come. We talk constantly, and I tell her how much I miss my family. When I grow sad remembering, she cheers me with some silly prank. She is changeable — sometimes exasperating — but I think Juan Pablo is right. She has a good heart.

But there is a dark side to my contentment. Fra Adolfo ordered me to report anything amiss in the household. It is my duty as a good Catholic to do so, he said. Yet I realize that I am becoming more comfortable in this home — and that I am less and less aware that the Delgados are Conversos. Everything I have seen suggests they are good people — and good Catholics. And then I realize, with a slight shock of surprise, that I am growing fond of them. What would Fra Adolfo say?

5

KEEPING SECRETS

Angelica does not walk. She skips, she runs, as if she cannot fit enough adventure into a day. One rainy morning she brings out her treasures, shells she collected on the beaches of Palos. "They were sea animals once," she explains. "Beautiful — yes?"

I hold each one, examining it closely, wanting to fix each detail in my mind so I may draw it. It is a wondrous thing to know there was once life inside. I think about my dead family. My memories of them are like these shells, something rare and beautiful left behind.

"I have never seen a beach," I say, fingering a spiral-shaped shell. "Or the sea. What are they like?" We are sitting on the floor of her room with her collection spread out on a black velvet cloth. From afar I hear the soothing bells of San Mateo.

"Never seen a beach or the sea?" she exclaims. "I will get Papa to take you with us the next time we go to

Palos! He cannot deny me. He never can!" She giggles. "And," she confides, "we are going soon."

"For holiday?"

"No. There is a man called Columbus who plans to sail away from that very port to find the Indies. That's where all the spices come from, you know. Papa says Columbus is fitting out three ships," she adds. "I do not understand it all, for what Papa says is that this Columbus believes the world is *round like a ball!* That if he keeps sailing in one direction, he will eventually come back to where he started. What a silly idea!"

"If the world was round, we would fall off," I say, trying to imagine living at the bottom of a giant ball. "What would hold us to the ground?"

Angelica shrugs. "Anyway," she rushes on, "we will see the ships and even get to board them because Papa must examine the sailors to be sure they are all healthy before they leave."

We have put away her shell collection and I am brushing her hair when I ask, "Will your brother come, too?" I try to sound merely curious, as if her answer means nothing to me.

She gives me a sly, knowing look. "Indeed. I will see that he does. But — there is talk . . ." Angelica lowers her voice. "Maybe I should not say. . . ."

I hold a hank of Angelica's curly hair and gently brush it.

"Can you keep a secret?" She looks over her shoulder at me.

"I can."

"Very well. But tell no one, especially Mama or Papa, because then they will know I have been listening to them when I should not."

"I promise."

She turns to me, her eyes large and serious. "One night, when Papa and Mama were talking, I heard Papa say that perhaps he should arrange for Juan Pablo to sail with this Captain Columbus. And Mama said she could not bear for him to go. That it would be too dangerous and it might be years before we see him again."

My throat tightens. I do not want Juan Pablo to go away. Though we have spoken only twice since that first day, I think of him often. "But why?" I ask, forcing the words out. "Why would your father want him to go?"

Angelica grabs my hand and squeezes it as I try to untangle a particularly difficult knot of hair. She does not answer my question for a time, but finally goes on when I put away the brush. "Papa says it would be good for him. He is skilled enough to be a ship's physician. But Mama says Papa is not fooling her. There are other reasons."

I cannot imagine nor have I the right to ask what those other reasons might be, but Angelica explains.

"Many of Papa's friends are leaving Spain. Maybe it has to do with that — I am not sure. Or — maybe it is because we are Conversos. The Church does not trust us." She shakes her head, frowns, and goes silent.

"Maestro Suarez will be here tomorrow," I say, changing the subject. "You have not practiced all week."

Angelica makes a sour face. "Margarita complains that she must cover her ears when I play. The cats yowl when I practice."

I laugh. "Margarita would not *have* to cover her ears if you practiced more."

"Some people do not have an ear for music," Angelica argues. "It is so unfair! Just because Juan Pablo plays well does not mean I can!"

Life is not fair, I think, but only say, "Nevertheless, you must try."

"Only if you sit beside me and help me read the notes."

"But Angelica! You know I cannot read music." I had hoped to use her lesson time to draw and paint with the new quill pen and ink, the black chalk and vellum paper that Angelica bought for me.

"I will show you how." She fixes me with a look that allows no argument. "Then, if I make a mistake, you will know enough to tell me."

"That would not be proper, Angelica! I am only a maid."

"So?" she asks. "How are we different? You are a maid because you were not born to rich parents, like me. You are my *friend*. That is all that counts, and the more we can share, the better friends we shall be. So — I command you, *friend,*" she says with a grin, "to sit by me and *help me*. Then the maestro will be happy, Margarita will not have to cover her ears, and the cats will not yowl when I play. Agreed?"

I laugh and choke back unexpected tears.

Serena and I are changing the bed linens in the room opposite Juan Pablo's when his door opens and he sees us. He crosses the hall and leans against the door frame, so casual and easy. He nods at Serena but looks directly at me. "And how are *you* doing, Maria Sanchez?"

Suddenly clumsy, I fumble with the pillow I am plumping, smooth back the hair falling over my face, and feel a weakness in my legs. "Well, thank you, Master Juan Pablo."

"And how goes it with my sister, the little angel?"

A smile trembles on my lips. "She has not yet grown wings, but she is trying," I say, surprised that I answer so boldly and that I dare meet his amused gaze.

"You must have a great influence on her, then," he responds.

"I think not. The little angel is teaching *me* things."

Juan Pablo makes a sound like he is holding back laughter. "Maria, you surprise me again." He smiles at me before he turns to leave.

For a while Serena and I continue our chores in silence, but I am disquieted. My head is full of questions I want to ask, questions Serena may be able to answer because she has been in the Delgado house for two years. I want to know if Juan Pablo usually speaks so openly with servants, as he did with me. I want to say, "He is so handsome and kind!" I want to ask, "Is he betrothed yet?" Marriages in wealthy families are often arranged long before the couple meet and for reasons other than love. But though I sleep in the same room with Serena, we are strangers. She spends much of her time in prayer and shows no interest in me.

So I am reluctant to speak — but suddenly she is not. "You must not speak to the young master as you did!" she exclaims. She pulls the down-filled comforter over the bed with tense hands.

"What do you mean?" I ask, though quite aware of my boldness. I take one side of the comforter and flap it to make it lie flat. "I only answered his question."

"You must not forget who *you* are and who *he* is."

"I *know* who he is," I say, hurt and angered by her words. "I meant no offense!"

"Nevertheless," she continues, "you are too free with the young master. It is not right!" She gives me a stern look, then retreats again into silence.

We move on to clean the next room, but her words remain with me. Did Juan Pablo think I spoke too freely? No. Serena is jealous! He addressed me, not her, and was amused by my answer.

On Good Friday, I attend early mass, as I often do, to pray for the souls of my family. I wear my new dress for the first time, and feel elegant as I make my way along the busy streets. For days Cáceres has been celebrating the coming of Easter with parades of priests and towns-people carrying huge crosses and statues of the Virgin Mother through the city. People line the streets, silent as the dead, as the procession passes.

The Delgados did not invite me to join them as Angelica had suggested. As I had hoped. It is a reminder that I am a servant, though Angelica calls me "friend."

Kneeling in the pew, I try to call up my father's body and face, ravaged by hard work and poverty, but his image is dim. Tears come when I think of my mother, her loving touch, the constant pain and acceptance in her eyes. And of Carlos, whose first spoken word was *Mama* — to me, not to our mother. I long to hold him, to ease the cough that wracked his frail body.

I have often seen Fra Adolfo at church services, but he has not drawn me aside to speak. Of that I am grateful, for I would not know what to say.

As I leave the church, a carriage draws up, the horses driven by Leon, a new man at the stables. He looks to be not much older than Juan Pablo. Dr. Delgado steps down and helps Doña Elena to emerge. Then comes the young master. He reaches a hand out to Angelica. They are dressed in their Sunday clothes, the men's boots finely polished. I watch from amongst the crowd, my eyes so drawn to the young master that I think surely he must sense my presence. And he does!

Unexpectedly he glances back, catches sight of me,

and smiles. Perhaps the gulf between us is not so wide as Serena says. Perhaps someday . . .

Walking carefully in my new shoes, I retrace my steps home, smiling.

6

A Forbidden Adventure

"Today is special," Angelica tells me as I help her don the dress she chooses, a simple gown of coarse material such as Serena or I might wear. "Today, we will have an adventure!"

I pay no heed to her words, for she is always planning some amusing way to spend the hours. I glance behind me into the open wardrobe that houses her clothes. "Which shoes would you like? The sandals? The slippers?"

"The boots," she answers. "We will need sturdy footwear."

I retrieve her heavy boots and squat to tug them over her small feet.

"I am surprised at you, Maria," Angelica chides, when I do not speak. "Where is your tongue? Are you not curious about where we are going?"

In the weeks that I have been Angelica's servant, I

have come to accept that though I am under orders to guide and protect her, it is she who decides what we will do, no matter how unwise. "Where *are* we going?" I ask, rising to my feet.

"Out." She reaches for her cloak and smiles mysteriously.

By "out" I assume she means the Delgado gardens, where we have spent many an hour together. We have played hide-and-seek in an orchard behind the house, beyond vineyards of wine-producing grapes. We have rummaged in toolsheds, examined potted plants in the glass-covered nursery, gathered armfuls of flowers, and tasted unripe grapes on the vines. She has even sat patiently while I tried to bring her likeness to life on the canvases she had bought for me.

She does not explain further about her plans until I have returned from my room with my cloak. It is then that she pulls on leather gloves and announces, "We are going into the *city.*"

She glides by me as if her words are of no consequence.

I try to catch the hood of her cloak. "Wait, Angelica! No! It is not safe. We cannot! Your mother would not approve!"

"Mama *never* approves — of *anything,*" she throws back at me. "She is like a cricket in a cage. I would rather *die* than live as she does, always afraid of what lurks around the corner!"

"Nevertheless, we must ask permission to go, Angelica!" I insist, remembering my orders to keep her safe. "We must!"

"Why?" she asks, her tone suddenly reasonable. "Papa and Juan Pablo do not need permission. They go out all the time, and no harm comes to them! Are men the only ones with the freedom to go where they please?"

"There is nothing worth seeing in the city, Angelica. Believe me. I know. I have seen it!"

She strides steadily down the long hallway with me right behind her. "Nothing worth seeing? So Mama says when we ride in the carriage to church on Sundays. But I hear different things from Papa. He says these are dangerous times. *How? Why?* I want to know. I want to see for myself!"

We start down the stairs. "Please, Angelica. Listen to me. It is not safe on the streets. There is much crime, and there are soldiers everywhere looking for trouble. Please, come with me. We will go to the orchards instead, and build a house in a tree as you wanted."

On the landing below I see Serena, on her hands and knees, scrubbing the tile floor. Can she hear our disagreement?

Angelica reaches the first landing and turns to me, face set in stubborn determination. "Do not argue with me, Maria. I will have my way! You know our city. You lived in it and no harm came to you, so how can it be so dangerous? Will you show me, or must I go alone?"

Serena, wet scrub brush raised, watches us as we move past her.

"Yes or no, Maria?" Angelica asks, forging on down the stairs.

My mind races. If I go to Doña Elena for permission, she will undoubtedly refuse. Knowing Angelica, she will slip away before I could return. If I go *with* Angelica, without permission, and am found out, I will lose my position. I have no choice.

"Yes," I say with dread. "I will go."

Angelica lifts a key from a nail near the kitchen door, and we slip out of the house. Willful child! She is at her happiest now, warning me to silence with a raised hand, running into the shadows around buildings, tiptoeing past the stables, where we hear a horse whinny, the scrape of shovels, the hum of men's voices. When we cross an open stretch of garden, Angelica slows her pace, as if out for a casual stroll. Finally she leads the way to a gate with a rusted padlock. She fumbles with the lock, but it will not give. She thrusts the key at me and impatiently commands, "You try!"

I manage to open the padlock and hand back the key. With great care we tug open the squeaky, long-unused gate and close it behind us. We are outside the Delgado compound, and no one saw us leave. I let out a deep breath of relief.

Angelica yelps like an excited puppy and flings her arms around me. "See how easy it is! You are such a good friend, Maria!"

I doubt that I am being a good friend by giving Angelica her way, but I am warmed by her trust and affection. Perhaps, if I show her only the parts of Cáceres where no harm is likely to befall us, all will be well. We start down the road together.

"You know what I wish to see, Maria?" Angelica asks, swinging our arms as we walk.

"What, young mistress?"

"Never call me *mistress!* It makes me sound so *old!* I am *Angelica.*"

I smile. "What — Mistress Angelica?"

She frowns at me as three horsemen trot by. They are bailiffs of the Inquisition! My legs grow suddenly weak. These men are to be feared. They have the authority of the Holy Office to search out infidels; they can stop *anyone* and bring him in for questioning. Happily unaware, Angelica waves to them.

"God help us!" I mumble a prayer and roughly grab Angelica's arm. "Never do that!"

She tries to struggle free, but I will not let her go.

"It is not seemly for a girl of your station to be abroad without protection! If they should stop to question us, they could do us great harm. They need no reason!"

"Have they ever stopped to question you?" she demands.

"No! Because when I walk through the city, I keep my gaze on the ground. I walk as a ghost, going about my business in such a way that I am not noticed. That is not to say that I am unaware! And if you go about the city today, you must do likewise. You cannot afford to arouse curiosity!"

Her voice is suddenly beseeching. "Do not be angry with me, Maria. I will do as you ask."

I release her arm. "Good," I say. "Now, where do you wish to go?"

"Do you promise to take me there?"

I hesitate, and with great reluctance promise.

She pauses, gives me a sly grin, and announces, "I wish to see the place where the Jews live — the Juderia."

7

TROUBLE

"No," I say, as firmly as I dare, because I do not feel confident to contradict her.

Angelica links an arm through mine and skips us along the road. *"Yes,"* she answers. "You must do as I say because I am your mistress. Besides, you promised."

How contrary! One minute I am her dearest friend, the next, her servant. I stop abruptly, face her, and say, "It is not allowed. Only Jews may go into the Juderia. The soldiers of the Inquisition watch those who go in and come out. Besides, the Jews do not like strangers in their midst. What if we are caught?"

"Allowed, not allowed," Angelica says. "Such rules have nothing to do with me. My father is physician to the Queen! I can do whatever I want!"

"We would be *noticed*," I rush on, hearing the sharp edge of fear in my voice. "Jews must wear a yellow patch on their shoulders. Do you not know this? Besides, the Juderia is crowded and smells different and . . . they do not worship Jesus and . . . they practice strange rituals. Some say the sickness started there!"

My words stop her but only for an instant. Her eyes narrow, and she gazes off into the distance, working out a solution to this problem. "We shall buy patches of cloth such as the Jews must wear and pin them to our cloaks at the shoulder!"

"I do not want to seem a Jew! I want nothing to do with them!" The very thought makes me shiver. "Why do you want to do this?"

"Maria! You just told me! That is the only way for us to enter the Juderia. Stop whining and lead the way."

Inwardly fuming, I lead Angelica to the Calle de Juderia, the market street of the Jews. It is near the walled ghetto in which they are ordered to live. Why this sudden interest in Jews? Has Angelica some connection with them that I do not understand?

The street is crowded, noisy, and smelly. It is lined with stalls whose merchants are selling all manner of things. Live chickens squawk and peck at seed in their cages. A goose runs between stalls to escape its owner. Peddlers hold up fabrics of cotton and silk and call out to buyers in a tongue I do not understand. Women pick over fruits and vegetables and argue over price with the farmers. Pots and pans are for sale, knives and table-ware, sheets and linens — even pungent spices laid out in colorful patterns on a wood table.

Angelica gazes about like a child at her first fair

and suddenly declares, "I know! I shall buy a chicken and bring it home for Cook to fix."

I stiffen at the silly plan. "How will you explain where it came from?"

"I will think of something." She darts among shoppers so that I must run to keep up, finally stopping in front of the stall where the chickens are sold.

After circling the cages several times, she points to one and cries, "That one! I want that one! The noisiest. We shall have it for dinner!"

The butcher is a bearded man with dark, deep-set eyes and a prominent nose. He glances quickly at our shoulders and as quickly looks away, coming to whatever conclusions a Jew might upon seeing two young Christian women shopping on this street. Carefully he opens the cage and reaches a gloved hand in to withdraw the chicken Angelica has chosen. The fowl lets out a loud squawk of protest. "Three maravedis," he announces, displaying the chicken for Angelica to see.

"One!" she counters, as if she has bargained all her life. Her eyes are bright with excitement.

"Three, young mistress," the butcher replies.

"One!" she returns with stubborn insistence. "Perhaps we should shop elsewhere!"

"Two, then," he replies, smiling. "You are a fierce trader."

"What do you think, Maria? Is that a fair price?"

"Yes, young mistress. I believe so."

She takes the purse hanging from her belt and

doles out the coins. With the air of one used to commanding, she says, "Prepare it."

In what seems an instant the man tests his knife, then slits the chicken's throat and drains the blood. Angelica makes a gagging sound and looks away. The vender hands me the chicken, still clothed in its feathers, seeming to recognize that I am Angelica's servant. I plunge it into the cloth bag I carry, and we move on.

Before we leave the street, we study the Jews we pass, especially the circle of cloth they wear. We stop at a fabric stall to purchase two such patches. The merchant eyes us with curiosity, and two boys in ragged clothes linger near, watching. "I have not seen you young ones before," the merchant says as Angelica pays.

"We are new to this city," Angelica replies, pinning one of the circles to the shoulder of my cloak, which makes me feel immediately uneasy and repulsed. "We are from Portugal, where Jews do not have to wear these . . . yet." Her voice is so guileless and her face so innocent that I would believe her if I did not know the truth.

"Welcome to our fair city, children," the merchant says. "And be sure you are within the walls of the Juderia before dark falls."

"This is so exciting! Now we seem like Jews," Angelica whispers, grabbing my arm as we leave the street. "I have always wondered what it would be like. What if I had been born a Jew instead of a Catholic?"

"Praise Jesus you were not," I say, pulling Angelica close to building walls to keep her from getting splashed by dishwater and slop being spilled onto the street. "And do not imagine that you are."

"*Now* I am Catholic," she goes on with great intensity, "but a long time ago, *a hundred years ago,* I was told, we were Jewish. Papa says it was a terrible time. His family *had* to convert. Catholics burned the Jewish quarter, and anyone who refused baptism was killed.

"I asked Papa why people hate Jews so much. 'For foolish reasons,' he said. Some believe that Jewish doctors carry poison in their fingernails. Some claim that Jews cut the hearts out of Christian children and use them in their sacrifices. Even priests say so. Can you imagine?"

Priests do not lie! How can Dr. Delgado question their words? I swallow my answer for fear of angering Angelica.

"And there is more," she rushes on. "People hate to pay taxes, of course. So who were appointed to be tax collectors? Jews! That makes it easy for people to hate them." Angelica strides along beside me and adds, "Papa says it is wrong the way people think. That Jews are much like other people. There are good ones and bad ones. Like good and bad Catholics. That is how to judge them."

I do not know what to think of Angelica's revelations. All my life I have always heard that those who are not true Catholics are evil. Why does Dr. Delgado speak as he does? Does such talk make him a heretic? I feel as if Fra Adolfo's cold gray eyes are watching me.

We are on a street near the walled Jewish ghetto. The narrow passage between buildings is like a tunnel because of the lines strung above, heavy with clothes drying. In earlier days the dark passage with its foul smells, much like the street where I once lived, would not have worried me. But today I am with Angelica, who is in my charge, so I feel uneasy. When I voice this fear, she points above us. "See the baby clothes drying?" she asks. "Families live here. They would not harm us."

Now that she wears the patch of the Jews, she is determined to enter the Juderia and see how the Jews live.

We are near the end of the dark, narrow street when I become aware that we are being followed. Glancing back, I see the two boys from the market who watched us so closely, joined by two others. I quicken my pace, pulling Angelica along as she chatters, unaware, at my side.

Suddenly I hear shouts and the pounding of feet running toward us. My arms tingle with sudden fear, and I drop my cloth bag. "Run!" I cry, giving Angelica a push. *"Run!"*

She glances back and, seeing the danger, puts on a burst of speed, with me at her heels. But we are not quick enough. Before we can exit the passage, the boys reach and encircle us. They are a ragged group, dirty and mean-looking, with knives in their belts. The smallest is thin as a stick, with the face of a rat. He is no older than twelve yet appears to be the leader. I try to protect Angelica, but she is yanked away, and in an instant, though I struggle, my hands are pinned behind me. "Jews! Swine! Ugly ones!" The leader spits in Angelica's face. "You will burn at the stake!"

"Leave us alone!" Angelica commands. "My father is physician to the Royal Court!"

The urchin laughs and in a high-pitched voice says, "And I am King Ferdinand! Your money or your life, pig!" The others laugh harshly as the leader tightens his grip on Angelica until she cries out.

"Do not hurt her!" I shout, afraid my protests are hopeless. "Her father *is* important!"

"A Jew — important?" The boy throws his head back in a loud, disbelieving guffaw. "Get her money, Manuel!"

One of the boys tears Angelica's purse from her belt.

I break free and fly at the leader, punching him with all the hate and terrified energy I feel. "Run, Angelica!" I scream as the others move in to grab me. I am hit and scratched, pinched and pounded until I think I will faint. A knife grazes my arm. Suddenly I hear a horse galloping up the street. In an instant the boys fall off and scurry away. I slip to the ground.

The horseman gallops by, unheeding, perhaps because the patch on my shoulder marks me as unworthy of help. It is Angelica who comes to my aid.

"Maria! Maria! Are you all right?" she calls, running back to me. She tucks her hands under my arms and tries to help me rise. "Oh, my! Oh, dear! You are hurt — and bleeding! It is all my fault!"

I stand and move to the closest building to lean against it. I am dizzy and unsure of my feet. Angelica fusses over me, wiping the blood from the knife wound on my arm. "Oh, this is terrible! What can I do?" I hear panic in her voice.

To ease her fears I say, "It is not so bad," and press a hand hard on the cut. "Bind it. Any cloth will do. Are *you* hurt?"

"Angry, not hurt!" Her voice is strong again. She reaches under her skirt and rips a strip of cloth from her petticoat. She ties the cloth around my arm and pulls it tight, all the while apologizing and begging forgiveness. "It is this hateful patch on our shoulders! They thought us Jews! Otherwise, they never would have touched us."

I do not answer, because what she says is true. I try my legs and limp a bit, leaning on Angelica until we come out into a public square. A carriage rumbles by. Three women stand near a fountain, talking. A carpenter fixes a door hinge. Two priests stride toward a church. Pigeons coo on a rooftop and swoop down to snatch crumbs. Someone must notice us, but no one offers help. With great effort and pain, I straighten and walk unassisted. "I can manage now," I say.

"We must go home at once!" Angelica exclaims. "Your wound needs care. It was foolish of me to bring this on you. Please forgive me!" She tears the patch from her shoulder, then mine, and pockets them. "How hard it must be to be a Jew. Thank God I am not!"

I know my wound needs tending, but I will tend it myself. How can I seek care from the Delgados? Questions would be asked. "How did this happen?" "Why was Angelica taken from the compound without permission?"

Angelica echoes my concern as we make our way home. "There is but one thing to do," she says. "I will go to my brother. I will tell him how it was my stubbornness, my willfulness that led to this trouble. I will tell him how you tried to protect me and that it is my fault that you were hurt.

"He will be very angry. I know that. But no matter how angry he is, he will forgive me because he understands this curiosity about Jews."

I nod, even though I find her comment strange. "But, Angelica," I argue. "He might tell your parents."

"Do not fret, Maria," she says confidently. "Juan Pablo will keep our secret. And he is almost a doctor now. He will know what to do."

I wipe away tears of relief. Strangely, through my pain I feel a twinge of excitement.

8

Juan Pablo Takes Charge

We are almost to the Delgado compound when we hear the sound of hooves galloping up the road. A horseman passes us, then turns and trots back. I gasp. The rider is Juan Pablo.

He reins to a stop. "Angelica? Maria! What are you two doing here?" he asks sternly. When he notices my bandaged arm, his voice softens. "You are hurt!"

Tears fill my eyes at his concern for me. "It is nothing," I say.

"I was going to come find you. We need your help." Angelica gazes up at her brother. "Ruffians attacked us, and they beat Maria. She has a cut on her arm. I bound it, but she needs more than I could do!"

"Why were you out of the compound? Where did you go?" He waits only a moment for an answer. *"Never mind!"* Juan Pablo leaps from his horse and strides to me. "You are limping, Maria. Is anything broken?"

"No! Just bruised, I think." I raise my hand to keep him from touching me.

He glances at the blood-stained bandage on my arm. "Come," he says, taking charge. "It is a distance yet to home. You must ride the rest of the way. You, too, Angelica!"

Without asking if I wish it, he lifts me as if I weighed no more than a feather and seats me upon his horse. I clamp my teeth together so as not to cry out at the pain. Soon Angelica is seated behind me.

"You must not tell Mama or Papa!" Angelica warns as Juan Pablo leads his horse up the road. "If they find out what we did, they will send Maria away. It is not her fault!" She goes on to explain how and why we left the Delgado compound, and she is true to her word: she tells him about the Juderia.

Juan Pablo does not answer in words, only with the fierce glance he throws back at his sister.

When we reach the compound walls, he lifts Angelica from his horse and leaves her at the locked gate that we slipped through earlier, for it would not be wise to be seen entering the grounds together. Alone, with key in hand, Angelica looks contrite and forlorn. "What will you do now?" she asks, seeming helpless for once.

"I will take Maria inside and examine her wound," Juan Pablo says.

"What will you say if Mama learns Maria is hurt?"

Juan Pablo thinks a moment. "I will say that Maria

was on an errand for you when she was attacked and that I found her wandering on the road."

"Oh, thank you, dear brother!" Angelica claps her hands together, eyes glistening with love. She smiles sorrowfully at me. "Again, Maria — I am so sorry."

Juan Pablo remounts his horse, settling in front of me. "Hold on as best you can," he tells me. "I will ride slowly."

Seated behind him, I press my cheek against his back and encircle his body with my arms. He smells of leather and soap. I am faint with the nearness of him, the pain in my arm forgotten.

It seems only moments before we reach the front gate. Roberto opens it for us, and we pass through to the stable. Juan Pablo dismounts, removes his leather gloves, and reaches to take me down.

"I can manage," I protest. "Really."

"Not until I am sure you have nothing broken," he says. Gently he gathers me into his arms so that, as he strides from the stable, our faces are so close that my heart nearly stops. I close my eyes and shiver, certain that he, too, must feel as I do.

"You shiver. You may be with fever," he says. "Roberto!" he calls. "Find Angelica. Call Margarita and tell her to bring blankets, towels, and my medical bag — at once."

He carries me to the music room and gently lowers me onto a leather couch. Then he stands above me, a frown of worry creasing his forehead.

"Please," I beg. "You make too much of this. If I may go to my room, I will wash the wound and rebind it. It is not serious. As for the bruises, I have suffered far worse." I struggle to sit up, embarrassed by his penetrating gaze, and try to stand, but my legs give way, and I fall back.

Doña Elena strides into the room as Juan Pablo settles me back on the couch. "What is this I hear from Margarita? Maria! What has happened to you?"

Juan Pablo tells his mother how I was hurt, and Doña Elena shakes her head in dismay. "Such lawless times! Where are the soldiers, those men with their lances and swords and fancy helmets who should be guarding our streets? Did they not hear you cry out? Why did they not come to your aid? Dios mio!" she exclaims. "They are too busy chasing Jews!"

"Mother!" Juan Pablo protests, glancing in my direction.

We hear footsteps, and Angelica comes running into the room, then slows when she sees her mother. Her face is flushed; she wears sandals and a fresh dress, having changed out of her muddy boots and soiled clothes. Margarita follows, carrying Juan Pablo's medical bag, blankets and towels draped over one arm.

"Please," I beg again. "This is not necessary. I feel much better now. I will go to my room and . . ."

Doña Elena cuts me short. "I am responsible for your welfare, Maria, and I will hear no argument. Juan Pablo will see to your wound and put salve on your bruises, and Dr. Delgado will check on you when he returns."

"Mama?" Angelica asks. "May Maria sleep in my room tonight? Then I can watch over her. If *I* were injured, she would do the same. Please?"

"Very well," Doña Elena says, "but enough talk. Let Juan Pablo do his work. Margarita, stay with Maria until she can be moved. Angelica, come with me! I want to know what purchase you thought important enough to send Maria into the city at this time!"

Juan Pablo's hands are gentle. He examines the bruises on my face, touching them softly, concern in his eyes. Without removing my clothes, he probes my stomach for pain and my legs for fractures. "Mother spoke of the many soldiers," he says, while he cleans the knife cut. His voice is gruff, and when I flinch at the pain, he gives me a look that seems almost tender. I close my eyes, sensing a powerful connection between us.

"They are without pity and more numerous than usual these last days, ever since the edict was proclaimed that by August, all Jews must leave Spain." He searches my face as if to gauge how I take this news.

"The Church is determined to cleanse our country of all who are not true Catholics. They are suspicious of everyone, even those of us who converted years ago." He bandages my wound, intent on what he is doing. After a time he adds, "Five infidels will be burned at the stake at the auto-da-fé next week. Did you see the scaffolds being constructed in the main square near the church?"

"No, I did not." I dare say no more in front of Margarita, and Juan Pablo gives me an understanding look.

The knife cut has left a gap that he silently treats with herbs and a styptic. He draws the two sides of skin together and while holding it thus tells Margarita to bind my arm tightly with a clean linen bandage.

"You have been very brave," he tells me when it is done. "I think the wound will heal with little scarring. Of course," he adds, as he puts his medical supplies away, "you should rest. Fortunately," he lays a gentle hand against my forehead, "you seem to have no fever."

Does he know what his touch does to me?

"When you feel better, perhaps you would like to draw — or read." He smiles.

"How do you . . .?" How does he know these things about me?

"Angelica has shown me some of your sketches of her. They are lovely. And she has told me that she is teaching you to read and that you are a good student."

I feel my face flush and hide it with my hands.

"Modesty is a good quality, Maria, but so is self-confidence. You should be proud of your achievement. Not many young women can read."

His words are unsettling — and inspiring. I vow to work harder to gain his favor and respect. "Perhaps I should go to my room now — to Angelica's room," I say.

"Indeed. Margarita will help you. And Maria? I will look in on you later."

As I lie on a cot in Angelica's room, I am overwhelmed by so many different feelings. The fear and pain of the attack, the guilt at deceiving Doña Elena — but most of all the strange and wondrous way that I feel about Juan Pablo. His voice, even in anger, gives me pleasure. A word of praise from him, and my heart leaps. Is this love?

Could it be — if I learn to read well, if I master the harpsichord so I may play duets with him, if I study Doña Elena's ladylike ways — could it be that he might see me as an equal and come to care for me as I care for him? I drift off to sleep smiling.

9

heResy in the house?

It is late afternoon when I wake up. Angelica hovers nearby. "How are you feeling, Maria? What are you thinking?" she asks, pouring water from a pitcher and setting the cup beside my bed.

"I am much better, thank you, and I am thinking I must never again let you have your way when I know the risks."

She ignores my declaration. "I am already planning our next adventure, so you must hurry and recover." There is such seriousness in her tone that I sit up in alarm.

She takes my hand. "Listen! Mother told me why I should not have sent you on 'the errand.'"

"Why?"

"Because of the auto-da-fé! There is much excitement in town, and much danger. Mama knows two of the people who will be burned at the stake — they were close friends a long time ago. She is terribly upset."

"If they are heretics, they must be punished," I say flatly. "The priests say that when we are baptized, we promise to follow Jesus only, yet these Conversos still secretly worship their God and practice their Jewish ways."

"No, no, *no!*" Angelica shakes her curly head vigorously. "You do not understand!"

"What do I not understand?" I ask, annoyed that Angelica, three years younger than I, thinks she knows better.

She sits down beside me on my bed. "Mama says that *anyone* can accuse someone of being a heretic — for the smallest thing, like not eating pork. Or fasting on a day that is not a Catholic day of fast. Or, or . . . wearing clean clothes on Friday night, as if this meant they would celebrate Jewish Sabbath."

"I know all this! The signs of Judaizing are announced each day in the streets!"

"Yes, but do you know what happens if you are accused?" Angelica shivers. "They torture you, Maria. The Inquisitors do horrible, cruel things to *make* you admit guilt even if you are innocent. I heard Papa tell Mama about a man he knows who was stretched on the rack until his arms and legs broke. I heard Cook say they force a stick into your mouth with nails on it!" She gags and covers her mouth. "Who would not confess to anything they ask to stop the pain? And then they burn the guilty at the stake, and the Church takes all their property. . . ."

I clamp my lips shut to stop from saying what I believe — that if a person is guilty, he deserves his fate. Heretics deserve to die. The Church says so. Infidels must be cleansed of their heresy.

Angelica must read my face, for she cries, "Where is your compassion, Maria! You cannot really think that burning people alive cleanses their souls? And what about the innocent who are wrongly accused?"

I can feel my resolve harden. No matter what she says, I believe the priests know best.

Angelica heaves a deep sigh and jumps up to pace the floor. "It seems to me we should all respect one another, no matter how we worship. What difference can it make?"

"Just what is your next adventure?" I abruptly ask Angelica, anxious to change the subject.

She hands me the cup of water. Some of the fiery enthusiasm of before is missing. "I want to see an auto-da-fé." She holds up a hand to stop my objections.

"Have you learned *nothing* from today?" I ask, incredulous. "You know your parents would never allow it!"

"We had trouble today because the ruffians who attacked us thought us Jews. We would go to the auto-da-fé as what we are — Catholics — so it would be perfectly safe."

"But it is horrible to see, Angelica! Why do you want to go?"

"Because. I am not just a silly child, as my brother and parents think. I hear things, but that is not the same as seeing for myself. If I were a boy, I would not be so protected. I need to know, Maria. Even if people do not believe as we do — how can they be punished so cruelly? Jesus teaches kindness and forgiveness. Why would Christians celebrate such a terrible thing?"

I avert my eyes, for I have a frightening thought. *Is it disloyal to talk like this? Is this what Fra Adolfo meant when he asked me to watch for signs of heresy?*

10

BITTER NEWS

In the two nights that I sleep in Angelica's room, we become like sisters. We chatter in the dark, sharing stories, with moonlight shining through the open shutters and the scent of summer in the air. "Were your parents like mine?" she asks the second night.

"My parents were very poor, but they loved me dearly. Papa was a big man but gentle. He tended sheep and sometimes stayed away for weeks," I tell her, holding the soft blanket close to my face for comfort. "Often the only food we had was bread and, if we were lucky, garlic and olives." I close my eyes, remembering, then add, "I always think of Mama scrubbing clothes or hanging them out to dry. Her fingers were rough and red, her nails torn. Still, I remember how soothing her hands felt when I was with fever and she stroked my head." I stop to swallow the hard lump in my throat. "They could not afford vellum paper or quill pens for the drawings I like to do. Mama dyed cork so I would have bright colors to work with."

"I like to watch you draw," Angelica says. "You seem lost in what you are doing."

I nod in the dark.

"And your little brother?"

"Carlos? I cannot even say his name without hurting."

There is a silence in the room, and I hug myself, remembering Carlos's big, frightened eyes as he lay dying.

"Maria?" Angelica asks after a time. In the dim light I see her leaning toward me on one elbow. "Are you still awake?"

"Yes."

"There is something that puzzles me."

"What?"

"I told you that my family were Jews a long time ago. They were forced to become Catholics, or die. So they converted. And ever since, the family married other Conversos who were also once Jews. So — am I still a Jew, though I worship differently?"

"Of course not!" I answer. "You love Jesus now, not the God of the Jews."

"Oh," Angelica says softly. "Is the answer so simple? I still do not really understand."

She is yawning now, so I make no reply.

After she goes to sleep, I lie awake. So many jumbled thoughts fill my mind. Is Angelica still a Jew, as she wonders? What a terrible thing that would be! Why do I dislike Jews so? Is it because the priests speak out so often against them in the streets and churches, calling them sinners? Saying they are stubborn and evil because they do not believe in Jesus? Is it because Jews live apart from the rest of us and dress differently? Because they are the ones who collect taxes and lend money at high interest? Yet — is it their fault? I think back to what Angelica said. Have the Church and the laws of our land forced them into such a life?

I am too confused to make sense of these thoughts, and finally sleep claims me. But soon I am startled awake by voices in the corridor.

"I think we must," a voice I recognize says. It is the master of the house, Dr. Delgado. There is pain and fatigue in his tone. I picture him in my mind: a tall, robust man with a dark brown beard, deep furrows of worry in his forehead, and eyes that show little emotion except when he gazes at his wife and children. "It would be a good time to go, Elena."

"We would take Angelica, too?" the Mistress asks.

"Surely. As things are, it would be best."

"And Maria? Angelica has become very fond of the girl."

I strain to hear the rest, but their voices fade as they move down the hallway.

What does it mean? Where are they going? And when? Am I to go, too?

In the morning, sunlight and sounds of activity in the hallway awaken me. At first I cannot remember where I am. Then I realize I am in Angelica's room. I wince at the pain in my arm, and when I turn in bed, I grimace at the ache from other bruises.

"Good morning, Maria," Angelica says, sitting up in bed and yawning. "Did you sleep well?"

"Yes." I smile at her. "And you?"

She stretches her arms out as if she would embrace the world. "I dreamed of sailing ships and distant places . . ." She looks toward the doorway and hops off her bed. "Whatever is that commotion?" Barefoot and still in her nightdress, she runs to the door and opens it. "Margarita? Serena?" she calls. "What are you doing?"

Through the open door I watch Margarita and Serena struggle by, each holding one end of a trunk. "Stop!" Angelica orders.

Serena's eyes meet mine.

"Your mother and father are going away, young mistress," she says dully.

"Without telling me? Where?" Angelica demands, amazed.

"I do not know, young mistress."

"Yes, well — go on, then." Angelica waves a hand in dismissal and closes the door. She moves swiftly to the wardrobe and I rise to help her. "This is so sudden and curious," she says. "Mama and Papa have said nothing about a journey. Hurry, Maria. We must find out what this is about!"

A few minutes later, Angelica races down the wide stairs to the dining room. I hurry to catch up with her. The Master and Doña Elena are seated opposite each other at breakfast. The table is set with a white cloth, fresh blue and yellow flowers, and platters of cold meats, cheeses, and fruit. I eat in the kitchen with the other servants, and our food is heartier and not so prettily served.

I sense that we are interrupting a serious conversation because the Delgados appear to be whispering. When they see us, they suddenly go silent.

"Mama? Papa?" Angelica says, sweeping into the room. "What is this I hear about a journey? Where are you going? Am I to go, too?"

"Is that the way to greet your Mama and Papa?" Doña Elena chides. "Come, sit with us, and we will explain."

Angelica gives each of her parents a kiss on the cheek and drops into a chair beside her mother while I stand apart, awkwardly awaiting instructions.

"Yes, we are going on a trip," Dr. Delgado says. "And of course, you are coming, too."

"Oh, joy!" Angelica says. She claps her hands in delight. "And Maria?"

"She, too." Dr. Delgado reaches for a biscuit in a basket on the table.

"And Juan Pablo?"

"Of course," her mother replies.

Angelica winks at me from across the table.

"When and for how long? And where are we going?"

"Tomorrow. To Palos. We will take a holiday — maybe a week, perhaps more."

"A *week*?" Angelica cries, a tone of disappointment in her voice. "*More*? But then we will miss the auto-da-fé!"

"Angelica!" Doña Elena exclaims.

"Little one," Dr. Delgado says seriously, "that is something you should never wish to see. And that is why we are making the trip now — so that we may all be safely away when it happens. It is a dangerous time to be in Cáceres."

"But . . ."

I shake my head slightly, warning Angelica not to plead.

Doña Elena notices me at last. "Ah, Maria, dear. How is your arm?"

"Much better, Mistress," I say.

"I am glad. While Angelica breakfasts, will you help Cook ready provisions for our trip? And then, if you feel up to it, give Margarita and Serena a hand, and see to your own packing?" Her tone is kind, but she is clearly dismissing me.

The kitchen is a flurry of activity. Two servants work at the ovens, where large loaves of bread are being baked for the journey. On the work table are cheeses, sausages, and fruits that Cook is wrapping. Two other servants are already helping, singing as they work. Cook shoos me off to be useful elsewhere.

Upstairs I find Margarita and Serena, who have already finished packing Doña Elena's clothes. They have lugged the heavy trunk out into the corridor, where some of the stable hands will carry it downstairs. We enter Juan Pablo's bedchamber together. It is a large, airy room with a balcony looking out on the vineyards and orchards. The wardrobe and dresser are of richly carved wood. The four-poster bed has a coverlet of Moorish design. A lute rests on a stand.

"The young master is particular about his things, so be most careful," Margarita cautions.

She calls off the items we are to pack: shirts and vests, trousers and capes, undergarments and boots. For one brief instant, when my back is turned to the others, I hold one of his freshly washed shirts close to my nose in hopes of breathing in his scent.

"Maria! Do not dream!" Margarita chides, striding to my side and removing the shirt from my hands. "We have much to do! See to his boots!"

And so it goes throughout the morning and into the early afternoon. Finally, I have only to pack my own few belongings. Then I will search out Angelica. I can hardly contain my excitement, for the only place I have ever known is Cáceres. What can it be like elsewhere?

I find Serena in our room, sitting on her bed, wiping at tears with her apron.

"Serena, what is it?" I ask, hurrying to her side.

"Stay away!" She holds up her hands as if to ward me off. Her voice is full of loathing. In the months that we have lived together, we have not become friends — but not enemies, either.

"What is it? Are you angry with me?" I ask.

"*You!*" She cannot even find words hateful enough to spill out her fury. She struggles for breath, then cries, "I have been here two years, and you only a few months! *I* should be going! Why you and not me?"

I recoil at the force of her anger, but understand it. She is jealous of my good fortune, and rightly so. "I do not know," I say softly, wishing I could find some way to ease her pain. "Perhaps it is because I am Angelica's servant. If this hurts you, I am sorry. Truly I am. I would not hurt you for anything." I move to the chest we share to choose the garments for the journey, guilt now tainting my joy at the coming trip.

Serena follows me, jostling my sore arm. "I know what you are after, Maria!" she cries. "But you will not have it! You *cannot!*"

"*What* am I after? *What is it* I cannot have?" I demand, spinning about to face her.

Red blotches spot her olive skin, and her mouth curls into a grim smile. "The young master! I have seen how you look at him. I know . . ."

"*What* do you know?" I ask, trying to sound unconcerned while my heart drums suddenly harder.

"More than you think! I am not dim, as they may imagine!" She shakes her head to emphasize her words, and there is an evil delight in her tone. "You imagine Juan Pablo will *marry you!*"

"How could you think such a thing?" I try to scoff and with trembling fingers fold my cloak, not daring to look at her.

She laughs, an unpleasant sound. "Liar! You already dream of it, I know! But beware. He will never marry you, never! He will have you, yes, if that is his will, but marry? You?" She laughs again.

I wipe my eyes with the sleeve of my dress.

"And do you know why?" she persists, positioning herself so she can see my face.

I want to run from her, run anywhere to avoid hearing more of her spiteful, poisonous words. Instead, I move away, choosing items to pack as if nothing she says can touch me.

"Do you know *why* he will never marry you?" she demands, following me.

"Why?" I whisper, with a sense of foreboding. "But you are wrong. I never dream he might."

Serena sits on my bed so that she faces me. The look on her face is gleeful. "Because you are like me. We come from *dirt*," she says. "And grand folk like the Delgados would never allow their sons to marry girls like us." She nibbles at a fingernail and watches me, a look of satisfaction on her face.

Her words are not surprising, for I have thought them myself, when I dare to dream.

"There is another reason, too." She spits a bit of

nail on the floor and looks up, as if expecting me to ask her what other reason there could be. I go on folding and refolding my dresses, not giving her the satisfaction. "He will never marry you," she gloats, "because . . ." She pauses to give the next words the greatest impact. "Because he will soon be betrothed to the beautiful Catherine Perreira. She is a Converso, too. That is the way with them. They marry their own kind."

"Is that true? Are you certain? When?" I ask. Serena merely smiles. Her malice is so deep that I know I could not expect true answers, anyway.

Did I ever really imagine Juan Pablo might love me, might want to marry me?

Yes.

Of course not. My throat fills with tears, but I summon up every shred of dignity I can manage and force a shaky answer. "You are mistaken," I tell Serena. "I am glad for Juan Pablo. Truly. And for the lady, Catherine, as well. I hope they will be very happy together."

11

journey to palos

That night I can hardly sleep, more troubled by Serena's words than excited by the prospect of the morrow. I cannot believe Juan Pablo is to be betrothed. Surely Angelica would have told me. I persuade myself that Serena made up the story to hurt me.

In the morning I feel hopeful. I will be traveling with the Delgados like a family member, seeing new places. Perhaps Juan Pablo will sit in the carriage beside me.

"Palos is not far," Angelica tells me as I help her dress for the day. "A four-day journey." She shows me a map, something I have never seen before. Maps are what travelers use to find their way from place to place, she says. It is a wonder to see. The whole of Spain — its shape, its mountains and rivers — are drawn on a single sheet of paper. Its great cities, such as Madrid, Toledo, and Seville, are but small circles within that drawing.

Rivers are merely lines. There are no people or trees, just words inside a shape. Angelica draws a finger along the line that is the River Guadalquivir. It flows by Seville until it reaches the Ocean Sea. "That is where we are going," she says.

The sun is just rising when the two of us leave the house to join the others in the courtyard. It will be hot soon, for it is late June, and we have not had rain for a while. The ground is dry and smells of dust. The shade trees wear dark leaves for want of water. The air is still; not even a small breeze touches us.

We find the carriage awaiting us, the trunks already loaded. Doña Elena, dressed in a blue traveling gown and wearing white leather gloves, is giving last-minute instructions to Margarita. Roberto and Leon, the new stable hand, are adjusting the bits on the horses.

Angelica squeezes my arm and nods toward Leon, a ruddy-skinned young man of medium height, with dark hair and dark eyes. "He watches you whenever we are about," she whispers. "I think he likes you. He is handsome — yes?"

"Perhaps." I am not interested in Leon or this line of talk, for I am distracted by Juan Pablo leading his horse from the stables. I realize, with a wrenching ache, that he will not be riding in the carriage with us after all, but following as guard.

"You may go now." Doña Elena dismisses Margarita and turns to us. The mistress appears cool and fresh and smells of roses, while I perspire in the growing heat.

"Ah, children." Smiling, she brushes the hair back from Angelica's cheek. "We should be on our way presently. How are you, Maria? Well enough to travel?"

"Oh yes, Mistress!" I raise my bandaged arm to prove my good health.

From the corner of my eye I see Dr. Delgado speaking with Roberto and Juan Pablo striding toward us. Heat rises to my face, and I straighten my skirt.

In a moment he is at our side, tall and elegant in his black riding clothes and shiny boots.

"Mother!" He lightly kisses Doña Elena. "And how is the little sister and her wounded guardian angel?" His glance goes to Angelica, then to me, and I see amusement and affection in his eyes.

If he is to be betrothed, why does he tease me? Serena *must* have lied. "I am fine," I answer softly.

"Son, help your mother and the girls into the carriage," Dr. Delgado says as he approaches. "Because of the Edict of Expulsion, the road to Palos will be swarming with Jews trying to leave the country. We should best be on our way."

Juan Pablo hands Dr. Delgado his horse's reins so that he can assist Doña Elena up the steep step of the carriage. When she is comfortably settled, he lifts Angelica in one great swoop. She kicks and cries out that she is entirely able to climb in herself. Then, smiling, he lifts me gently while asking after my arm and saying that he will see to changing the dressing at our first stop.

At last we leave the compound, with Roberto and

Leon controlling the horses pulling our carriage. The Master and Juan Pablo take up positions in front and rear, as guards.

At first we three women do not speak, occupied by the jostling movement of the carriage and by the changing scenery. I cannot help but smile as I lean forward to see from the window all that we pass. Once we have left the city behind and taken to the main road, we pass small farms and hill towns, large olive and pomegranate groves, endless vineyards, and *people* — more than I could ever count. They stream down the road and slow our progress. We press handkerchiefs to our noses to avoid the dust they stir up.

From my seat in the carriage I look down on wagons loaded with mattresses and household goods pulled by bearded men. Women carry babies in their arms and heavy sacks over their backs. Little children stumble along, some clutching crude toys. Above the sound of movement we hear voices raised in a singsong — like prayer?

They are all Jews. The yellow patches they must wear on their shoulders almost glow in the bright sun. They look exhausted and dispirited, as if they have walked for many days from great distances.

Juan Pablo spoke of the Edict of Expulsion, but I want to know more. "Why are they being expelled?" I ask the Mistress. "And where are they going?"

I can see by Angelica's sudden attention that she also wants to hear what her mother will say.

"Queen Isabella and King Ferdinand ordered all Jews to accept baptism or leave Spain by the first of August. Most would not give up their religion. A leader of the Jewish community, a man named Abravanel, pleaded with the monarchs, reminding them of the hundreds of years of friendship and peace Spain has enjoyed with the Jews. He offered to donate a large sum of silver and gold to the state — as much as 600,000 crowns — if only the Jews could stay."

"That is a great deal of money!" Angelica exclaims.

"Yes. But the Chief Inquisitor is said to have appeared just as Abravanel made this offer. The Inquisitor was furious. 'One People, One Kingdom, *One Faith,*' he cried, holding up a crucifix before the King and Queen. He likened the offer to a bribe. He said, 'Behold the Christ whom the wicked Judas sold for thirty pieces of silver.' The King and Queen had no choice. They could not cancel the edict."

"Where will the Jews go, Mama?" Angelica asks.

"Africa, Holland, the Ottoman Empire, Portugal — though not there for long, I think. There is talk of a marriage between our monarchs' daughter and the son of the Portuguese king. If that takes place, Spain will demand that Portugal evict its Jews, too."

"I am sorry for them," Angelica says. "It must be so hard to leave the place that has been home for so long."

"Yes," Doña Elena agrees. "And with such short notice. Only four months to sell homes and businesses. I hear that some have traded their properties for a goat or a wagon — and sometimes not even that. It is a shame, really — a terrible shame." Doña Elena pulls the curtain covering her window and fingers the cross around her neck.

"It is so very sad!" Angelica says, snuggling against me for comfort.

I put an arm around her shoulder, as if in agreement, but my mind spins. All my life I have been taught that the Jews are infidels, people to be reviled, not pitied. That as long as they remain in our country, they are a bad influence on those who *did* convert, people like the Delgados. Could the King and Queen be wrong? And the Church?

12

helping the enemy?

As the day progresses, the heat becomes unbearable. Dust seeps into the carriage unless we keep the curtains closed, and the air inside grows stale. No longer do I care about the passing scene or bother to converse. Doña Elena sits staring ahead, waving a fan before her. Angelica slumps against my shoulder, asleep, and I dare not move for fear of waking her.

We stop at last, just off the road, in a grove of trees. Juan Pablo, his cloak grayed by the dirt of the road, helps us down, one by one. Stiff from the long, jostling ride, we stretch and breathe in the fresh air, then take cool draughts of water from his goatskin. Nearby, on the road we have just left, the Jews move on like a thick line of ants. It is hard to take my eyes from them. Their flight both fascinates and repulses me.

While Leon tends the horses, Roberto lays out rugs

for us to sit on and brings Doña Elena the basket that Cook prepared for our repast.

It is a goodly feast that I help the Mistress set out — several kinds of bread, sliced meats and cheeses, olives, wine, and fresh fruits. So much more than my family ever enjoyed.

When I rise to join Roberto and Leon, who take their meal under another tree, Doña Elena motions for me to stay by patting the ground beside her.

I heap a plate, eager to enjoy the bounty. But then, a short distance away, I hear a child cry. It is a hopeless, constant wail, like that of one so weak with hunger it is close to the end. It is the same sound my beloved Carlos made when he lay dying. I cannot eat, for the food sticks in my throat.

"Can we do anything?" Doña Elena asks.

Juan Pablo rises. "Perhaps I can help. Father, may I go?"

"They are Jews," the doctor replies quietly. "You know the law. But — yes, go."

I hold my breath. Though I may not be familiar with recent edicts, even I know that befriending or even helping a Jew in any way is an offense severely punished.

"Take Leon with you," Dr. Delgado says. He glances to where Roberto and Leon are napping and adds, "Never mind. Take Maria. Should you need anything, send her back for it."

But it is against the law, I think in fear, even as I rise.

And even if it were not, even though I am sorry for their child, *I want nothing to do with Jews!*

"I want to go, too!" Angelica exclaims, leaping up beside me. But her father fixes her with such a stern look that she sits back down.

"Take water and what is left of our food," says Doña Elena, already wrapping up the cheese and sliced meats.

Juan Pablo strides ahead, carrying a goatskin of water and his bag of medical supplies. I carry the sack of food and hurry to keep up as we climb a slope toward the family with the crying child.

"It troubles you to be doing this," Juan Pablo states, glancing at me. "Why? Because it is against the law?"

I think for a long moment how to answer, not wishing to earn his disfavor. But finally I say, "Yes. And because when my little brother was dying, no one came to help him, and he was not a Jew."

"I am sorry about your brother. If I had known, I would have tried to help."

"The priests say the Jews . . ."

"Ah, the *priests,*" he says with disdain. "They say many things — that when Jewish doctors treated Christians, they killed one of every five patients. That Jews caused crops to fail and plagues to flourish." He scowls. "There is a Spanish proverb — 'Only the blind fail to see and the deaf refuse to hear.'"

"What?"

"Where is the Jesus of infinite mercy, of compassion toward the justly and unjustly afflicted? Does it not seem to you that Jesus would want us to help someone in need, no matter who he is, no matter what his religion?"

"But the Church says — "

Juan Pablo stops abruptly and turns to me. "Go back, Maria. I would not want to put you in danger or have you do what is against your beliefs." His tone is flat, and for the first time since I have known him, his eyes are cold.

I flinch at his disapproval. "No — you are right. I am sorry," I hurriedly reply. "I will come." But the damage has been done. A breach that never existed before lies between us now.

The family of Jews has settled far back from the road. The father bends over an old woman leaning against an orange tree and wipes her brow. The mother walks slowly back and forth, cradling her crying infant and whispering desperate prayers while two children sleep on a straw mat and a third sits listless, watching. They are startled by our approach and immediately begin gathering up their few belongings, as if to flee.

"*Shalom!*" Juan Pablo calls out in greeting. My heart nearly stops, for I have heard men greet each other that way near the Juderia. Does Juan Pablo know other words in the Jewish tongue? Would Fra Adolfo consider this a sign of Judaizing? I shudder at the thought.

"Maria, give them the food," Juan Pablo says, offering them the goatskin of water.

At first, doubt and fear show on the parents' faces. Then the father's eyes fill with tears, and he accepts our offerings with much mumbled gratitude.

"I am a doctor," Juan Pablo says. "May I see your baby?"

The woman gives him the tightly wrapped infant, and he lays it on a rug on the ground. Juan Pablo is very good with the child, undressing it, cleaning its soil with rags the mother gives him, then swabbing its overheated little body with cool water.

"Will he take your milk, Mother?" he asks gently.

The woman shakes her head as if she feels ashamed and responsible for the illness. Juan Pablo nods. "You must do this," he instructs, looking up at her. He removes a clean cloth from his bag, pours two or three drops from a bottle onto the cloth, and holds it to the baby's mouth. "This will calm him," he explains. "Then you must see that he takes water. It is most important. A little each time, drop by drop. And do not wrap him so warmly." Rising, Juan Pablo corks the bottle and hands it to the woman.

"Where are you going?" he asks.

"To the port of Palos," the father replies. "To find a ship."

"Have you any money?"

The man hesitates, as if fearing Juan Pablo might steal what maravedis he may have, then explains, "The day we left our village, we were set upon by thieves who stole all we had of value."

"Then how will you . . . ?" I ask, knowing they will need money to buy passage. Juan Pablo throws me a warning look before I say more.

"We will manage, young miss," the father says. "God will provide."

"Safe journey, then, sir," Juan Pablo replies. He slips some coins beneath the loaf of bread we leave behind. "Come, Maria."

"Thank you, kind sir," the man calls after us.

We walk away quickly and do not speak. Juan Pablo seems preoccupied, as if he has forgotten that I am with him. I wish he would explain how he knows the Jewish greeting. Could it be he has connections with Jews? I feel uneasy in his presence, and cannot look at him.

"Will the baby live?" I ask, to break the silence.

"I think not. He has lost a great deal of fluid and cannot hold down food."

I think of how I felt when Carlos lay dying, so helpless and lost. "How will *their* God provide?" I ask, thinking of all the times I prayed for help in vain. There must be something in my tone that offends Juan Pablo, because he frowns at me as if he thinks me both unkind and stupid.

"They believe God cannot be everywhere at once, so man must help do God's work," he says. "When that family reaches Palos, they will find money for passage

— maybe not from God, but from other Jews. It is the custom of these people to help those in need. Does that answer your question?"

There is so much disdain in his voice, such dislike that I am embarrassed and do not know how to reply. I busy myself climbing over rocks, trying to keep up with him. "Would they not be better off if they had converted?" I ask finally.

"If you were told to renounce your religion or leave Spain, which would you do?"

I open my mouth to answer, then close it. Does he think the Church is wrong in the way it treats the infidels? If I had to leave my country or convert to another religion, of course I would leave. But this is different. These are *Jews!*

Still, the baby's cry echoes in my ears.

13

at the house of perreira

Toward the end of the day, while Angelica and Doña Elena talk quietly to each other, I gaze out the carriage window, thinking. What did I say to make Juan Pablo change his opinion of me so suddenly? How can I regain his affection and respect?

What meaning should I give to the sympathy and caring the Delgados show to Jews? To Juan Pablo's understanding of their language and their ways? To Angelica's questions about her family's history and her curiosity about Jewish life? And why do Conversos almost always marry other Conversos? Is it to maintain their connection to their heritage?

Are the Delgados Judaizers?

It takes my breath away to even imagine such a possibility. I tell myself it cannot be.

For three days we move steadily and slowly south, taking rest at night at the homes of Dr. Delgado's Catholic friends. Angelica tells me that they speak with anguish about the eviction of the Jews. Although it is dangerous to question the Church's authority, some challenge its campaign against Conversos and its cruel methods.

By the fourth day I am eager to be on solid ground again. The long hours of constant jostling have tired me, but we are approaching the seacoast now, and I feel revived and excited. The air feels heavy and moist and smells of brine. Now the road is choked with carriages, and I wonder, with the crush of people, where we will sleep this night. At another of the doctor's friends? At an inn? I hope not, for what I know of them is not pleasant. Fleas live busy lives in filthy beds, and nights are noisy with drunken voices.

I should not have worried. Late in the afternoon the carriage climbs a steep hill, with olive trees on each side of the road, to a huge stone castle. We ride into the inner courtyard and descend from the carriage as a nobleman in velvet breeches and silk shirt strides forward. Waving his hat in a graceful sweep, he bows and smiles greeting. A plump, pretty woman follows with a girl older than Angelica but perhaps younger than I at her side. The girl is beautiful, so beautiful that I step back, awed and subdued. Her hair is the color of copper and her skin as pale and smooth as cream. But it is her eyes that set her apart. Unlike any I have ever seen, they are almond shaped and green.

I stand apart as the Delgados embrace what appear to be old friends. The master of the castle, Don Miguel Perreira, announces, "And you remember our dear Catherine." He gestures to the copper-haired girl.

Catherine? The name rings in my head like a glass shattering. This must be the Catherine that Serena spoke of, the girl she said Juan Pablo would marry! Catherine Perreira! So it is true after all.

I listen and watch as if from a distant place. Juan Pablo steps forward and bows before the girl. She smiles sweetly and curtsies. Angelica claps her hands, and all the parents beam.

While Roberto and Leon tend the horses, we are led inside the castle to a great room with ceilings so high they echo our voices. I follow in a kind of daze, not knowing what else to do. In the flurry of greetings, I was overlooked, and I feel out of place.

Angelica falls back to walk beside me and whispers, "She is beautiful, yes?"

I swallow the huge lump in my throat and mumble, "Yes."

"Do not be sad, Maria. This should be a happy time, for while we are here we will celebrate the betrothal."

Celebrate the betrothal! How can I not be sad? Why did she keep this a secret from me? Tears sting my eyes, and I tremble with anger. Juan Pablo flattered me. He made me believe he really cared for me. Even Angelica made me think he found me attractive!

I want to run off to a dark corner and cry. Surely Angelica must understand my feelings. But she moves away from me — to talk with Catherine.

I stay in the servants' quarters of the castle. Angelica and I do not dine together or spend much time together the next day. At mealtime I take food with the other servants in the kitchen, a large room with a huge fireplace, shelf after shelf of dishes, huge kettles and pots hanging from hooks, and a long trestle table that could seat twenty. The food is plentiful and good, and the conversation lively.

"I have not been north in fifteen years," the cook muses. "What is it like these days?"

"Bigger, noisier," Leon says.

The stable hands ask about the feed given the horses and other livestock back in Cáceres.

Two of the maids tell us woefully of their young men, who have signed up to sail with Columbus in the next week.

The groundskeeper says that Palos is bursting with Jews. "They are like weeds waiting to be plucked from this soil and cast elsewhere to root again."

I listen to their conversation but remain distant from it, angry and envious. My thoughts keep returning to Juan Pablo. I am furious that I let myself believe he admired and cared for me when all the time his thoughts must have been on Catherine and their coming betrothal. As for the Jews — I am tired of hearing about them. Let them leave my country if they will not be true Catholics.

"You are so quiet, Maria." Leon addresses me from across the table as conversation bubbles around us. "Is there anything wrong?"

"I do not speak when I have nothing to say," I reply.

His ruddy face grows dark, and he busies himself spearing the meat on his plate. I am instantly sorry to have spoken so rudely, for he only meant to be kind.

"Forgive me — I am out of sorts," I say, trying to make amends. I pause, surprised at the thought that enters my head: *I miss my family*. "Perhaps you *can* help. I should like to find my uncle, my only living relative. He commands a ship, but I do not know its name, or its whereabouts."

"What is your uncle's name?" Leon asks.

"Francisco Sanchez."

"A common name. Do you know anything else about him?"

"No. I met him only once, five years ago. I remember a man of great girth, a bulbous nose which I liked to tweak, and twinkling eyes. Other than that, I know little that would be of help."

"There are more vessels than usual moored in the harbor to accommodate the Jews who are leaving. I shall inquire in town."

"Thank you, Leon. It is good of you to do this," I say, appreciating his kindness.

"It is nothing." A whisper of a smile plays on his lips as he dips a bread roll into the gravy.

After dinner Angelica seeks me out, and we explore the castle gardens. It is a place riotous with deep red bougainvillea. Crickets and bees sing their songs, and there is an overwhelming perfume of flowers. I am just beginning to feel comforted by all this beauty when Angelica tells me that the marriage bans will be announced in church on Sunday. I hardly have time to take in this news before we round a hedge and see Juan Pablo and Catherine ambling toward us, hand in hand. He whispers something to her, and she laughs. Catherine's duenna follows a short distance behind.

I want to turn and run, but my legs are like pillars of stone.

"Ah," Juan Pablo says, bowing to us without smiling. "Catherine — you have not met Angelica's guardian, Maria."

I curtsy but feel ugly and awkward before her.

"Welcome to my home, Maria," Catherine says.

"In the short time she has been with us," Juan Pablo continues, as if praising a clever child, "she has learned to read and play the harpsichord better than my sister. And I have seen some of her drawings. She has an artist's eye and skill."

I scream silently, for he exaggerates greatly and speaks of me as if I were not present. As if I am a little child. As if I have conquered some feat that everyone in his world takes for granted. I am so angry and hurt that I can barely look at him.

"We were just going to my father's library," Catherine says to me. "I want to show Juan Pablo a new book Papa has acquired. *The Prison of Love,* it is called, by Diego de San Pedro. Have you heard of it?"

I shake my head, eyes downcast, for I feel helplessly inadequate. Not only is Catherine beautiful, but she is learned, too, while I can only read simple texts and play uncomplicated melodies on the instrument Juan Pablo claims I play so well.

"Come, Maria," Angelica says, taking my arm. "There is something I wish to show you."

My legs move on by force of will. Angelica, for once, falls silent.

We stop, finally, outside a small building with a beautifully carved door. "It is the castle chapel," Angelica says. "You go in first."

The space is small and intimate and smells of incense and candles. Angelica and I are the only ones there. Dark paintings of angels and saints and Jesus line the walls. The altar is of carved wood in gold leaf. It is where the Perreira family worships, Angelica whispers.

Angelica and I kneel to pray. My heart still aches from the recent encounter. I think of Fra Adolfo and the frightened child who sat in his office just a few months ago and know I should feel grateful for my better life. How foolish to want more than I was born to. It should be enough that I enjoy the warmth and friendship of this good family. *But I do not feel grateful,* I think to myself. I am envious and bitter. And angry with myself for feeling so.

After a time I open my eyes and gaze at the intricate stained-glass windows, lit by a row of thick candles on a table below. I see saints and cherubs, scenes from the Bible, stars such as light up the sky at night. Many stars, some oddly shaped.

Suddenly my eyes return to a particular window with six-pointed stars. Strange. A sudden memory comes vividly to mind.

I am nine years old, sitting on Uncle Francisco's lap in our small home. Uncle is telling Mama and Papa about his travels to distant lands.

He collects flags, he says, of every place he goes.

"Of France and Italy? Of Greece and the Ottoman Empire?" Papa asks.

Uncle nods. "Even of cities." He pauses, then adds, "Once I saw a flag of the Jews from a place called Prague. A strange flag that had a star with six points and a hat in the center. The emperor gave the Jews in that city the right to have their own symbol on a flag. Gold and red, it was . . ."

The six-pointed star is the sign of the Jews? Why is it on this window, in this chapel, in the House of Perreira? Are they Judaizers? And if so, what does this say about the Delgados?

For the first time I allow such a question to linger in my mind.

14

so many secrets

Night is falling as Angelica and I make our way back to the castle. "I saw six-pointed stars on the window in the chapel. Is that not the Star of the Jews?" I ask Angelica this less from curiosity than from a desire to hurt, because the news about Juan Pablo still stings.

Angelica hesitates, and the look she sends me is surprised and perhaps a little fearful. "The six-pointed star? A Jewish symbol? I do not know. I did not notice. This is a former Moor's castle, deeded to Don Manuel after the Moors were defeated and banished from the country. Perhaps they were responsible for the design. What I do know is that Don Manuel is a good Catholic and much valued at the Royal Court for his cleverness with money."

"Umm," I say, only half-satisfied with her answer. And I think, as the priests say, that Jews are clever with money.

Angelica excuses herself then, saying she wants to go to her room and read. She is polite but distant. I think of all the times we read together in Cáceres. Would she call me her best friend now?

In the next few days, Doña Elena, Angelica, and I — sometimes accompanied by Catherine — explore Palos. It is swollen with Jewish families frantic to leave Spain before the Edict of Expulsion is final. One can smell the fear and anguish in the streets, especially along the quay where the ships are moored. We walk cautiously among the throngs, not wishing to touch or be touched. Doña Elena is sympathetic. She says these people face great hardships even before they reach their new homes in strange lands — rough seas, sickness, pirates, and crews who will rob them of their few valuables or kill them.

We visit the shops in Palos for things not available in Cáceres. I go along, but Angelica clings to her mother as we move from shop to shop. There is much to buy: gold jewelry, paintings, and beautifully embroidered linens that the Jews have bartered in their last desperate efforts to raise money for passage.

"No," we hear a shopkeeper declare to an elderly man and his wife as we examine a showcase. There are the low, desperate mutterings of the old man and the harsh voice of the shopkeeper. "No! I have no market for these. Go away! I have bought all I will from you Jews."

When we walk along the docks, gulls screech overhead and drop like arrows to the water to spear fish. I am entranced by the beauty and mystery of the sea, yet it is spoiled by the reality. It is shocking to see sailing ships so crowded with passengers that it seems incredible they stay afloat. Here I feel the greatest longing for my own roots, my own family. Here I think again of my sea-captain uncle and wonder if he might be commanding one of these vessels.

One day Dr. Delgado invites us along when he visits Columbus's ships to examine the sailors and inspect the food supplies laid in for the long journey. It is a special treat, he says, and we must not get in the way, although he jokes that such pretty women will surely distract the crew in any case.

The *Santa Maria* is the larger caravel of the three ships going on the long voyage to the land of spices. We watch from the quay as provisions are loaded. Angelica reads aloud the words on the cases and barrels — wine, salt pork, sardines, cheese, lentils, beans, garlic, honey, almonds, and raisins. The sailors are bearded and barefoot, wearing short, loose-fitting garments and red stocking caps. It is hot and terribly humid. I hold my nose, for the stench of dead fish, sweat, and garbage nearly makes me retch.

Captain Columbus is a tall man with hair that was once red, I am told, but is now gray. He is a deeply religious man, Catherine says. While preparing for the journey, he stays at a monastery nearby with Diego, his son.

He bows to each of us and greets Doña Elena with special warmth. But it is clear his mind is elsewhere as he calls orders to one or another sailor. While Dr. Delgado goes below with the captain, a sailor shows us about, explaining the plan to sail west across the Ocean Sea to the Indies and return with the pepper and other spices and goods that countries want. It is all very puzzling to me.

When I ask how they can figure the time and how far they travel each day, we are told about the ship boys, called "grommets." They move the sails that control the vessel's direction and speed. They measure time by watching sand sift through a tiny hole in an oddly shaped glass. Each time the bottom of the glass fills, they turn it over and sound a bell. Eight turns equal four hours; every four hours a watch ends, and the crew changes.

After a few hours we women have seen enough and are wilting from the heat. We cluster together, doing our best to keep out of the way of the sailors while we wait for Dr. Delgado to take us ashore. Still, a sailor carrying a heavy crate on his shoulder accidentally jars Angelica. While Doña Elena comforts her and the sailor apologizes, the Master emerges from below. Columbus is at his side, and they are speaking in low tones that I overhear.

"You will consider it?" Dr. Delgado asks. "It would be a service to your crew, a good experience for him, and a relief to me that he is abroad in these troubled times."

"I will consider it."

Dr. Delgado nods solemnly. "Then I will return for your answer tomorrow. Let me say again that I would be most grateful — and generous — if you are able to do what I ask."

My heart nearly stops. Dr. Delgado is talking about Juan Pablo! Pleading that Columbus take Juan Pablo with him! It seems such a foolhardy and perilous voyage, sailing off the edge of the world to where serpents and terrible sea creatures could swallow up their small crafts. Why would Dr. Delgado risk his son's life when he could be safe with his family, in Spain?

Again that night, Angelica and the rest of her family dine with the Perreiras, while I eat with the other servants. At dinner Leon reports that he has made inquiries about my uncle but has no news of his whereabouts. I do not even know why I put him to the trouble, except that I feel less and less a part of the Delgado family and hunger for a connection with my own people, even an uncle I hardly know.

Angelica summons me to her room after dinner. Her eyes are bright, her face flushed. She pulls the door behind me. "Maria! Papa wants Juan Pablo to go with this man Columbus!"

I say nothing about what I overheard and already guessed and help her undress for bed.

"Papa and my brother had a terrible row. Juan

Pablo would not hear of leaving. He has never *ever* spoken to Papa as he did!"

"What did he say?" I take her shoes and turn my back so she cannot see my face.

"That he would not go! That nothing would change his mind! That Papa exaggerates the dangers of the Inquisition to Conversos who are faithful to the Church. That even if there *is* danger, how could Papa expect him to leave Spain and abandon his own dear family? Mama and I could hear their loud voices through the study door!"

I am glad Juan Pablo refuses to leave, for I do not want him to go. As angry as I am with him, I would miss his attention. But then I have a bitter thought. Why, really, does he want to stay? For Catherine? Can he love her so much that he cannot bear to leave her?

"But what of the betrothal? The wedding? If he should go, would Catherine wait?" I ask. "The trip with Columbus is full of risk. And there is no telling when he would return."

Angelica stiffens. "Juan Pablo did not speak to that. He only said that though we are Conversos, we are good Catholics, and the Church is not after people like us. We *are* good Catholics, are we not, Maria?"

I hang her dress in the wardrobe and nod. After days of keeping her distance, she is suddenly my confidante again.

"Mama cried!" Angelica continues, returning to the overheard conversation. She climbs into bed. "I could not console her. She hates to hear Papa and Juan Pablo argue. 'When all the Jews have left Spain, things will be better,' she insists. But Papa claims she has her head in the sand. He says that when the Jews are gone, the Inquisition will bear down even harder on the Conversos."

Angelica presses a hand to her mouth as if suddenly remembering something. She stares at me, as if measuring my trustworthiness. "Oh! Mama said I am not to speak of this to anyone — not even you, Maria! At times like this no one is to be trusted. Not even close friends.

"But that is silly!" She frowns. "If you cannot trust your best friend, who can you trust?"

15

A HORROR AWAITS US

It has rained almost constantly the last several days, and I wish we were back in Cáceres. Dr. Delgado goes off to Columbus's ships each day, but for me there is little to do. I wander the many damp halls of the castle, feeling lost and miserable. Angelica spends most of her time with Catherine now, Doña Elena with Catherine's mother. When we are together, Angelica sings Catherine's praises until I want to strike her, but I smile politely instead. When I see Juan Pablo with his betrothed, my heart aches. He is so enamored that he barely nods to me.

After the wedding bans are announced on Sunday, the Perreiras celebrate with a grand party. I watch from a window as ladies in their finest gowns and gentlemen in fitted black pants and scarlet capes arrive in their carriages. They embrace the Perreiras and Delgados, then disappear into the castle. Music floats across courtyards to the servants' quarters, where we also celebrate. Wine flows, and there is much food — pastries filled with cheese and spinach, pots filled with flan layered with honey, huevos hominados, and all kinds of fruits.

Leon asks me to dance, but I turn away, unable to enter into the festivities. My mind rages with images. Catherine in a dress the color of her eyes. Catherine with fragrant jasmine woven into her hair. Catherine dancing with Juan Pablo.

Suddenly Leon touches my elbow. "I have learned something about your uncle," he announces. I try to interrupt my obsessive thoughts, but I am only half-attentive.

"He is at sea," Leon continues. "Captain of a ship called *La Gran Esperanza*. They say he is returning to Spain soon — that is, if he is the Francisco Sanchez who is your uncle."

"Gracias," I say, moving on.

"De nada," he calls after me.

I should be more grateful to Leon. And I should be happy about the news of my uncle. But right now all I can feel is my misery.

I have come to hate this place. The dampness, the heat, the loneliness, the rejection. I want to go home!

"We leave tomorrow," Doña Elena informs me a few days later. This means it is my task to do the packing and to help Leon and Roberto carry the trunks to the courtyard. Juan Pablo has prevailed in his debate with Dr. Delgado. He will not sail with Columbus after all.

The trip home is much different from the journey to Palos. Doña Elena and Angelica huddle together, discussing the wedding plans most of the time. I am left out, for they whisper as if they do not want me to hear. I pretend not to notice and stare out the carriage window.

There is an endless tide of Jews on the road, flowing in a direction against us, though fewer now than two weeks ago. They are as dreary a mass of humanity as I have ever seen. Earlier I felt little sympathy for them, but now that I, too, feel rootless, I can almost understand their loss.

The several days we spend traveling in the carriage seem endless. At night, when we again stay with Dr. Delgado's friends along the route, Angelica does not seek me out.

On the stifling afternoon that we approach Cáceres, Juan Pablo rides up to the carriage and peers in at us. "Is something wrong?" Doña Elena asks.

"The auto-da-fé was postponed because of the rain," he reports, studying his mother's face. "It is being held today."

Doña Elena presses a gloved hand over her pursed lips. She frowns and glances anxiously at Angelica. "What does your father say?"

"Father says we will try to avoid the main streets. There is sure to be drunken revelry. He thinks it best to pull the curtains so you will not see or be seen."

Angelica grasps her mother's arm. "I want to see what is happening!" she cries, as her mother draws the curtain and orders me to do the same on my side of the carriage.

"No, Angelica!" There is a note of fear in Doña Elena's voice. "People go mad when there is an auto-da-fé! You cannot predict what they will do! Just pray that no harm comes to us!" She nervously fingers her prayer beads.

As we enter the city, I glance at Angelica, wondering if she is now thinking, as I am, of her plan only a few weeks ago to attend the auto-da-fé, despite my objections. How strange that the Delgados left home to avoid the event, yet fate has ordained they be here nevertheless.

A low drone of voices swells to a roar with each street leading us closer to the Plaza Mayor. Though I should not, I peek around the curtain and see people leaning out of windows, waving banners, shouting and laughing. The streets run with a crush of crazed men and women pushing toward the plaza.

On one street corner a monk reads aloud the Edicts of Faith. I know by heart the list of ways to recognize Judaizing, for I have heard them so often: working on Sunday and resting on Saturday, refusing to eat pork, wearing a small amulet around one's neck with a parchment inside in Hebrew that reads, "And thou shalt love the Lord thy God with all thy heart and all thy might . . ." And on and on and on. . . .

Closer to the plaza we are stopped by a procession of black-cloaked and hooded monks. The lead monk carries the banner of the Inquisition. Behind them come dignitaries in colorful uniforms and church officials followed by armed soldiers guarding the accused. It is easy to tell which are prisoners, for most wear Sanbenitos, large vests painted with devils and flames, and ridiculous cone-shaped hats. They are barefoot and carry candles. Taunting citizens crowd close to the accused, whipping them with switches and pelting them with rotten fruits and vegetables and foul-smelling slime.

Doña Elena closes her eyes, fingers her rosary beads, and recites Hail Marys. Angelica ignores her mother's orders and peeks from the window.

Bells ring and drums roll, and the procession surges forward to the Plaza Mayor. There, I know, are the platforms for the dignitaries and the accused, for I have seen this spectacle before. Soon, citizens of Cáceres will crowd the plaza, cheering on the ceremony. Each prisoner's crimes will be announced and a sentence proclaimed. Those who refused to admit their Judaizing or to reveal names of others will be strangled and burned — or burned alive.

I shudder at the prospect, for it is a terrible sight, even if burning cleanses the soul, as the Church says. I am revolted to the core. Angelica sits rigid, as pale as death.

When we reach the Delgado compound, we are all somber. In silence Juan Pablo helps each of us from the carriage. When he lifts me, his hands are not gentle as before. He does not even look at me.

16

under suspicion

There is a new atmosphere in the house of Delgado, different from only a few weeks ago. One I do not understand or like. One night, during dinner with the other servants, I dare speak of this to Leon. "Do you notice a change in the Delgados?"

"What do you mean?" he asks.

"Before we went to Palos, there was laughter and openness. Now, it is as if the whole family is holding its breath — waiting for something. They seem guarded, like they trust no one except each other. Angelica is so quiet. She hardly tells me anything. It is as if I am no longer her friend, only her *servant*." I hear my voice choking on the word "servant."

"But you *are* her servant, Maria. Did you ever think otherwise?" he asks. "As for me, I see no difference — for I have little to do directly with the family. I know my place."

I dislike Leon for his bluntness and am angry at myself for speaking so freely. I crumble a piece of bread between my fingers so I do not have to look at him.

Cook overhears our conversation and pulls up a chair to join in. "Maria is right. There is fear in the house. With the wedding ahead, one would think the family would be happy."

Roberto looks up from the soup he is slurping. "They are troubled by the auto-da-fé."

"What of it?" I ask.

"The Delgados are Conversos."

"So?" I ask again.

"The accused are *all* Conversos," Roberto says.

I must digest this for a moment. Then I say, "But the Delgados have been Catholics for the last hundred years! They cannot be under suspicion!"

Roberto shakes his head. "That does not matter. More and more Conversos are being called in and questioned. The Church believes that no matter how long ago they converted, many are infidels and secretly practice their old religion. The chief inquisitor, Torquemada, is determined to wipe out all Judaizers."

Cook adds, "No Converso can feel safe these days." She glances around and lowers her voice. "Every day soldiers bring more of them in for questioning." She shrugs. "If I were tortured in the ways I hear about, I would name anyone the inquisitors suggest — even my own mother — to stop the pain." She turns to look at me. "What would you do, Maria?"

Rather than answer I argue, "But Dr. Delgado is physician to the Royal Court! Surely he is above suspicion!"

"No one is above suspicion — not if accused. If you do not like a Converso, accuse him. If the Church wants his land and his money? Accuse him. That is what some believe, I hear — that the Inquisition is not so much about glorifying the faith as it is about taking Converso property."

"But," I protest weakly, "the Delgados are good Catholics!"

"They are *Conversos*. Once they were Jews, so they will never be trusted. Their blood is tainted. The Inquisitor demands all Catholics to be of 'pure blood.'"

For days after, I think about these things and in my mind go over the litany of signs to identify Judaizers. Are any of these signs in the Delgado home?

Lately Fra Adolfo watches me whenever I attend services. His small, probing eyes search my face so that I feel faint with guilt that I have not brought him the information he seeks. What could I tell him if he asks me questions?

And then, a few weeks after our return from Palos, I receive a message. It is delivered by a nun who asks to speak with me in private. It is a summons from Fra Adolfo, an order to meet with him.

"Why?" Angelica asks, when she learns of the request. Fear shadows her face. "What could he want? Why would he ask to see you?"

I shrug, as if I do not know, aware of a certain satisfaction that I, too, can be secretive.

"What if he asks about us?" She sits tensely, watching me, waiting for my response. "What would you say?"

"What is there *to* say?" I slowly answer.

17

I reveal too much

With Doña Elena's permission, I leave the compound the next morning to see Fra Adolfo. I cannot forget that I made a pact with him. In exchange for the privilege of working in the Delgado home, I was to report any transgressions of faith.

It is like a pact with the Devil, I realize.

It has been months since I left him to live with the Delgados. Then, I was too desperate, too hopeless to be afraid. Now, at the prospect of this meeting, I am full of fear.

What will he ask, and how will I answer?

I slept little, for all night I thought of how I would respond. I made myself remember how the Delgados took me in when I was so in need and made me feel welcome. For that I am grateful. But then I made myself dwell on their recent slights and rejections. Fickle Angelica, who treats me like her friend only when it suits her. Juan Pablo, who once seemed to care for me and now ignores me. The Master and Mistress, who led me to believe I was one of their family and now remind me of my true position — as servant.

Hurt eats at my heart like a hungry worm, and I cannot stop it.

Fra Adolfo's office is as I remember: dim, smelling of dust and old sweat, cluttered with books and papers. A desk faces the door, and gray light seeps in through the one window. My eyes fix on a knotted leather strap hanging from a hook on the wall. I am reminded of stories Papa told about the priest. That he beats himself regularly with such a strap to cleanse himself of unclean thoughts and desires. I wonder what those thoughts and desires might be.

This time, instead of keeping me waiting, he looks up immediately when I enter his office. "Ah, my child," he says, as if pleased to see me. "You look well. The Delgados must be treating you kindly." He motions me to take the chair near his desk and dismisses the nun who brought me to his room, then folds his hands and leans forward.

"It is time we talked. I had hoped you would come to me on your own, without my summons."

I look away, not knowing how to answer.

"I have followed your progress at the Delgados and have received nothing but good reports."

"Thank you," I whisper, leaning back in my chair,

for his breath smells of garlic. "The Delgados are kind to have said so."

He nods. "They — and others."

Others? Serena? Margarita? Who else in the household would report on me to Fra Adolfo? If he already knows that things go well at the compound, why am I here?

"You were in Palos with the family recently. Yes?" His gray eyes narrow.

"Yes," I say.

"The purpose, of course, was for Dr. Delgado to examine the sailors on Columbus's ships?"

"Yes."

"And the son — Juan Pablo — became betrothed to another Converso?"

"Yes," I reply with a catch in my voice.

"Did you hear or see anything amiss before that visit or since?"

A flutter of fear runs down my arms, and I glance at the strap. I know what he wants. Though this is my chance to hurt those who hurt me, I cannot.

"Speak, Maria Sanchez. Do not be afraid." Smiling encouragement, Fra Adolfo strokes his nose with his fingers. I notice that his nails are cracked and bitten to the flesh. "Do the Delgados follow any of the practices banned by the Edicts of Grace? Shall I remind you what they are?"

I shake my head, for those edicts are imbedded in my mind as deeply as memories of home.

"Do they ever communicate with or sympathize with Jews, or secretly meet with other Conversos? Tell me everything you know, child!" he wheedles, almost in a friendly manner. "It is your duty!"

I must give Fra Adolfo something. Something unimportant, perhaps. But suddenly I cannot stop the pain in my heart from spilling out.

"On the way to Palos, we stopped to rest near a Jewish family with a sick baby," I tell him. My throat tightens as I recall Juan Pablo's scorn — his harsh words when I said it was against the law to aid a Jew. Breathless, I rush on. "Juan Pablo greeted them in their language and helped them. Is that what you mean?"

The priest's eyes gleam, and he nods, pleased.

"Doña Elena knows a Converso who was convicted and burned at the stake. Is that what you mean?"

He nods again, yet there is something in Fra Adolfo's eyes, a narrowing and sly probing, that almost stops me. Eagerly he leans forward. "Yes. Go on."

For a moment I hesitate, frightened at what I have said. I am crying now, digging my nails into the palms of my hands to stop myself. Yet I stammer, "In Palos, Dr. Delgado begged Captain Columbus to take Juan Pablo with him. Why? Is he afraid the Inquisition will learn of Juan Pablo's sympathy for Jews?"

The priest smiles, entwining his fingers, his eyes never leaving my face.

I wipe my eyes, out of breath. I think how secretive the family has become since the auto-da-fé. How I float through their house like a ghost they do not see. Why have they changed toward me?

But I have said enough — *too much.* "That is all, Fra Adolfo. No more."

The priest leans forward, no longer smiling. "Then I shall help you. Where were you just before Easter, when the Jews celebrate their Passover?"

I search my memory, but find no word such as "Passover" there. I stare blankly at Fra Adolfo.

"Do you remember being given a free evening? The other servants as well?"

I am puzzled, wondering where he is leading. Then I remember. "Yes. We were all given a free evening a while ago. Some went into town, but I stayed in my room to practice my reading."

"Reading? But that is against . . ." He stops himself. "No matter. Tell me, child. That night, did you hear any strange music, perhaps, or chanting — anything out of the ordinary?"

"No."

"Ah, well. Was there any unusual food prepared?"

I suddenly recall a curious thing. The best dishes had been laid out in the pantry, as if for important guests. Perhaps the Delgados were preparing for company, but if so — would they dismiss the servants? As quickly as the thought surfaces, I bury it. I have said too much already.

Fra Adolfo sees my hesitation and is about to probe

further when there is a rap on the door. "I am not to be disturbed!" he shouts.

"Concentrate, Maria!" he insists, his gray eyes boring into me. "There are reports of Judaizing in the Delgado house. What else do you know?"

Perspiration rolls down my neck. "Nothing! In the name of Jesus, Mary, and Joseph, I swear — nothing!" I am suddenly terrified. What have I said? *What have I done?*

"The Delgados are good Catholics," I stammer, trying to make amends. "Good people. Not Judaizers, no. Who could say otherwise?"

"You realize, child," he says, in a threatening tone, "that it is a crime to protect those who betray our true religion."

"I know." I bite my lip and shudder. I could not bear being tortured, having a rag plugged into my mouth, choking on water poured down my throat. I force myself to hide my thoughts and shake my head vigorously, repeating, "No! Nothing more."

And yet he persists. "On Friday nights, I stand on a hilltop and look down on the homes below. If smoke does not rise from a chimney, I am sure those inside are Jews, for Jews will not light fires — not even candles — after dark on the Sabbath. Nor will they work once the Sabbath begins, for it is their day of rest and worship. Do the Delgados light fires on Friday nights?"

"Yes," I say. "Always!"

He is not pleased at this answer, and though he questions me further, I will add nothing more.

Finally he rises and with barely controlled irritation says, "Well, Maria, I must trust you have told me everything. But I expect more when you visit me next." His eyes narrow again. "I am convinced that Dr. Delgado and his family are guilty of Judaizing. If I am right, they must be cleansed so their souls might go to heaven."

I run from the church, stumbling over the cobblestone streets, tears stinging my eyes. Along the way I must stop, lean my forehead against a wall, and spew up everything in my stomach.

When I reach home, torn by feelings of shock and guilt at what I have done, I find Doña Elena at her sewing. There are dark circles under her eyes, as if she is not sleeping well. She asks me nothing as I pass by.

Serena is in our room reciting the rosary, her spirit so far away, it seems, that she does not even notice me. Is she the one who tells Fra Adolfo what is happening in the Delgado home? Would she invent stories that would hurt the family because they did not choose her to go to Palos? Would she speak out of spite?

Soon after my return, Angelica calls for me. "What did he want?" she asks when I enter her room. She sits on her bed, hugging her knees, biting her lip, looking like a frightened little child. I knew she would ask me that question and worried how to answer it as I ran home.

I study my fingers. "He asked if I am happy in my position here."

"Is that *all*, Maria? You were gone so long!" she cries.

I hesitate, then admit that he asked if the family ever followed any of the practices banned by the Edicts of Grace.

Angelica's face loses all color. She draws in her breath and stares hard at me. "And what did you say?"

I think of all the things I told Fra Adolfo that could be used against the Delgados, and feel ill again.

"I said that you are good Catholics," I tell her, straightening her bedclothes so I do not have to meet her gaze.

She leaps off the bed and hugs me. "Oh, thank you, Maria! Bless you! I was so worried!"

I squirm against her undeserved, loving embrace.

Two nights later there is a loud pounding on the front door. I spring upright in bed, clutching the bedclothes to me, afraid to believe what I dread.

Serena whispers hoarsely, "What can that be?"

We wait and listen, barely able to breathe until we hear Roberto call out "Who goes there?"

The pounding continues.

"Who goes there?" Roberto repeats, louder, above the pummeling.

"Soldiers of the Inquisition! Open the door, on orders of Tomás de Torquemada!"

I gasp and bite my thumb, staring in terror at Serena. Soon we hear loud voices and the clanking of armor.

"We have orders," someone calls out. "We are to take Dr. Eduardo Delgado in for questioning! He is to come with us at once!"

Oh, Judas. What have I done?

nowhere to turn

I press my fist against my mouth and spring from bed. This is the consequence of spilling my confusion and fear out to Fra Adolfo.

I pull on my robe and run down the hall to where I can see and hear better. In the entrance hall I see five soldiers facing Dr. Delgado, Doña Elena, and Juan Pablo. Several servants wait in the shadows.

Angelica, in her nightdress, cowers on a low step of the staircase, eyes wide with fear. One of the soldiers, his helmet gleaming in the candlelight, binds Dr. Delgado's hands while Doña Elena clings to her husband, sobbing. The doctor's face is pale and blank, as if he cannot fathom what is happening to him.

I hurry to Angelica and put an arm around her, murmuring meaningless words of comfort. This is a terrible, terrible thing for the Delgados.

"How dare you?" Juan Pablo shouts. "My father is

physician to the Royal Court! He is faithful to the Church and the Crown! You will be severely punished if you do not leave at once!"

The soldier yanks at the rope around Dr. Delgado's wrists, ignoring Juan Pablo's protests.

"Oh, husband! Oh, dear husband! What shall we do?" Doña Elena cries. "What shall we do?"

"Calma, Elena!" the Master says, regaining his composure. "I have done nothing wrong. They cannot keep me."

Soon, with two soldiers on each side of him, he is pulled forward and out to the courtyard, where a horse waits to carry him away.

Those of us watching are silent with shock. Doña Elena buries her face in Juan Pablo's shoulder, shaking with sobs.

I am frozen with horror and guilt. Truly, I did not mean for this to happen. If only I could take back what I told Fra Adolfo!

"I will go to Torquemada immediately," Juan Pablo tells his mother, "and demand that father be released!"

"But what if they detain you as well?" she cries. "How will we manage without you *and* your father?"

I stroke Angelica's head with an icy hand, sick with fear.

"I must go, Mother," Juan Pablo insists. "Have courage. Be strong!" He calls for Leon to saddle his horse.

Doña Elena finally wipes her eyes and orders the

servants back to their beds. "Maria," she tells me, "Angelica is frightened, and she takes such comfort in your presence. Please stay with her tonight."

"What will they do to Father?" Angelica asks as we whisper long into the night.

"They will ask him questions — that is all," I lie so as not to alarm her. But I shudder. They will torture him to make him confess. They will force water down his throat until he chokes. Perhaps they will hang him by his arms until they pull out of their sockets. They will whip and burn — No! I must not think of what they might do. I must fill my mind with hope. Perhaps, because of his position or Juan Pablo's intervention, he will be released.

"Angelica!" My voice rises above a whisper when I suddenly remember the patches she bought to allow us to enter the Jewish quarter. If the soldiers return to search the house for signs of Judaizing, finding the symbol of the Jews could destroy the family. "Angelica! Did you throw away those patches you bought from the Jews?"

"Why?" she replies. "I kept them to remember our adventure. They are in my cabinet." Suddenly she realizes why I asked and cries, "Oh, Maria! If they come back and find them!" She leaps from her bed and yanks open a drawer from which she pulls the badges of the Jews. She thrusts them toward me. "Destroy them!"

I seize the candle on her dressing table and hold

each to the flame. While the circles of cloth curl into ashes, I wonder if there are other symbols in this house that could tie the Delgados to their past.

It is mad, this searching out of every possible little transgression of faith. How mad my own blind hatred of Jews now seems. The Delgados are good people, people who care about others. Does that not count?

Angelica and I spend the morning hours with Doña Elena, awaiting Juan Pablo's return. The Mistress lies on her bed with a wet cloth on her forehead, staring at the ceiling.

"Mama," Angelica says, as gently as she can. "Maria said the soldiers might search our home. Is there anything at all they might find that would make them think we are Judaizers?"

"Nothing!" Doña Elena says, rising from her bed in distress. "Nothing, I tell you! Our family has not practiced that religion for a hundred years!"

I turn to the window, so full of guilt I fear my face will reveal my feelings. "He is back," I announce from the window seat where I can see the road leading to the house. "Juan Pablo has returned!"

Moments later he strides into the room, dusty and haggard from the strain of the long ride. I can tell that he does not have good news. Doña Elena holds out her arms to him. "How is your father? Have you arranged his release?"

"I am sorry, Mother. I could not see the Grand Inquisitor. No matter what I said or threatened, they would not let me see Father, either. I was told he is being questioned, that informers — they will not say who — have identified him as a Judaizer."

Juan Pablo's voice breaks. "Imagine! We, who go to church regularly, who believe in Jesus, are treated as infidels! I ask myself again and again — who could have spoken against him? Could it be someone in this house?" His eyes widen as he looks my way, and his voice becomes cold. "I understand you spoke with Fra Adolfo yesterday, Maria. What did you say?"

I shrink at his reproach, though I deserve his wrath. "Nothing!" I cry. "There is nothing *to* say!"

He stares at me a moment longer, then turns back to his mother. "I will try to reach the Queen. Surely she will speak in Father's defense! Meanwhile, we must pray and hope for the best. They will release him soon," Juan Pablo says with conviction. "They *must!*"

My heart breaks when I hear the pain that Juan Pablo cannot keep from his voice. Hurt and envy drove me to turn on the Delgados — but I never imagined it would have this effect. I must go to Fra Adolfo and recant. But the prospect of facing him again terrifies me. What if he refuses to believe me now, or sends me to the Inquisitor? What if I could not withstand the torture? Would I say whatever they wanted me to say?

I hurry to the church while the family rests in the afternoon, anxious to return before being missed. But I am told that Fra Adolfo is away, not due to return until tomorrow. I beg the Mother Superior to avow to the priest that I lied. That Dr. Delgado is innocent of any transgressions of faith. That I would swear on my life it is so. That the things I spewed out came from resentment, not from truth.

I ramble and repeat myself and finally break down in tears. The Mother Superior listens patiently, puts a kindly arm around my shoulder, and assures me that she will speak with Fra Adolfo when he returns.

I trudge home, more anxious than before, unaware of anything around me. Even if Fra Adolfo returns in time, I believe he will do nothing. *Nothing.* He hates Conversos as much as he hates Jews.

What of your own prejudice, Maria? Look what it has led to!

I search my mind for what I can do to save Dr. Delgado. But if Juan Pablo can do nothing, what could I, a lowly servant, do?

19

JUAN PABLO SUMMONS ME

Angelica's trust makes me even more ashamed of my deceit. She clings to me now, depending as she once did on my advice and company. In turn I assure her, without believing so, that all will be well.

The next afternoon I slip away again to find Fra Adolfo. I will retract everything that I told him earlier. I am ready to *beg* him to trust Dr. Delgado, regardless of what anyone said. But when I reach the church, a priest turns me away. "Fra Adolfo will not see you. He says there is nothing more to discuss."

Juan Pablo rides out each day in valiant attempts to arrange his father's release. He seeks out men in high places to swear that his father is above suspicion, but none has the courage to do so for fear of also becoming suspect. Angelica confides that he even bribes those who might give him access to their father, but to no avail. It is a dark time in the house of Delgado, and it is I who brought the darkness.

Then, suddenly, a week later, Dr. Delgado returns.

"My darling!" Doña Elena cries, rushing out to the courtyard to greet him. "Oh, what have they done to you?"

His hair, only days ago a deep brown, has turned stark white. His face, thinner and deeply creased, is like that of an old man. Although he attempts a smile, he is clearly in pain, for he presses one hand to the opposing shoulder. With a cry of anguish Angelica runs to her father and throws her arms around his waist. Juan Pablo rushes to help him.

Praise God that he is alive! I close my eyes and silently offer thanks.

The family retires to the salon and closes the doors. I do not know what they discuss, for I am not invited to join them. Is the danger over? Dr. Delgado's release must mean that he has been judged innocent. I am so relieved. It is as if a heavy stone has been lifted from my heart. I need to share my joy and fears, but with whom?

Leon is in the barn, currying Dr. Delgado's horse. For a moment I watch him before he sees me. He has a sturdy body, well muscled. His movements are sure and firm. His attention is focused entirely on the gentle black mare, to whom he whispers softly.

When he hears my footsteps and looks up, his face breaks into a cautious smile. "Ah, Maria," he says, continuing his grooming. "And what can I do for you?"

"Did you see Dr. Delgado, how terrible he looks?" I can hardly speak, suddenly close to tears when I imagine what the Master must have gone through. "But at least he is home." A horse in a nearby stall whinnies, and I wonder if it is as sorrowful as I.

"I saw him," Leon says grimly. "And it is not yet over. They will interrogate him again and again, until he breaks."

"He will *never* break!" I cry, not because I believe what I say but because I could not live with myself if he did. "Not the doctor! He would never incriminate anyone, especially family, just to save himself!"

"Believe what you will." Leon returns to brushing the mare. "But do not count on it. I am a practical man and look ahead. If he is condemned, the Church will take over this house and everything in it. We will all be looking for work."

"How can you care about *that?*" I demand, aware that others may hear us and lowering my voice. "What of Angelica and Doña Elena and — and — Juan Pablo, and how they will suffer?"

"Ah yes, them," Leon says as if they are really of little interest. He smooths a gentle hand along the horse's flank and does not look my way. "Do not judge me too harshly, Maria. I am not uncaring, but I must think of my own future. As you must think of yours."

I choke at his words. How can he be so cold? Is it my interest in Juan Pablo that goads him?

"And why are you here, Maria?" he asks, putting

aside the brush and offering a handful of oats to the horse. "For further news of your uncle?"

Although that was not my purpose, I nod and wipe my eyes with a corner of my apron. In fact, standing here before Leon at this moment, I wonder why I did come. To share my burden of guilt? No, I dare not admit my deceit to anyone!

Leon cleans his hands on a rag and studies me. "I have no other news than what I told you in Palos. But I will do what I can to learn more."

He comes closer, concern in his eyes. "Why do you weep, Maria?" With one finger he traces the wetness on my cheek.

I want to scream, "I have done a terrible thing! I am the one who betrayed the Delgados! I am the reason they came for the Master!" I ache so to confess, yet I keep silent, burying my self-hatred like a seed in my heart.

When Leon puts his arms around me, I do not resist. But he is no comfort. He mistakes my tears as pity for Dr. Delgado and fear of the future.

"Do not worry, Maria," he murmurs. "If the Master is condemned and we must leave here, I will take you with me. You must know how I feel. . . ."

His words are so unexpected and unwanted that I thrust my arms out to put distance between us. "Please, please!" I shake my head. "This is no time to speak of such things!" As long as I feel so unworthy of trust, I cannot think of making a life with any man.

When I leave Leon, I am more troubled than before. He believes the Inquisition has not finished with Dr. Delgado. If that is true, then the whole family is in danger.

The threat of disaster, like a storm about to break, weighs heavily on us all. The Master takes to his bed and is little seen. Doña Elena stays close by him. Angelica moons about, taking solitary walks, showing none of her usual sparkle. The servants are on edge, quick to anger and complaint. I have put aside my artwork, lacking inspiration and desire. I dwell on what to do to help the Delgados.

One night in our room, Serena says, with a kind of smug satisfaction, that she will return to her family in Valladolid "when the Master is burned at the stake."

"How dare you?" I scream, shaking with fury, though it is I who caused this calamity. "He is not guilty! He will not be burned at the stake!"

"Who are you to tell me what I dare say, O High and Mighty Maria?" Serena spits back. "I know more than you think. Look at you — the pot that calls the kettle black!"

"What?" I sputter, shocked at what she implies.

"When the Master is burned, I am off to Valladolid, as I said."

It is all I can do to keep myself from striking her. I leave the room to stand outside against the wall, trembling.

The next day, after Maestro Suarez has given Angelica her lesson, she remains at the harpsichord playing melancholy chords while I sit beside her. "They will come for Father again," she says. "Juan Pablo is certain."

"Perhaps not," I counter, without conviction.

"He says they are gathering more evidence, calling in each of the servants, threatening Papa's friends to declare untrue things about our family." Her voice breaks, and she looks up at me with sorrowful eyes. "When they have enough evidence, they will come again."

I swallow the lump in my throat and put an arm around Angelica. She falls limp against my shoulder. "Oh, if only I could do something," she whispers. "But what?"

The same frustration fills me. "I wish I knew," I say, aware again of my deceit.

Later, I am thinking of my conversation with Serena when she finds me helping in the kitchen. "The young master asks to see you in the library," she announces with a knowing smirk.

What could Juan Pablo want? I press my hand to my chest as Doña Elena does when in distress. Has he learned of my deceit? Cold sweat begins to trickle down my back. When I first came to work here, Doña Elena asked three things of me: hard work, honesty, and loyalty. I have worked hard, but in honesty and loyalty I have failed miserably. Am I to be dismissed? Is this why he asks to see me?

I suck in my breath and try to regain calm. Juan Pablo said the Inquisitors do not reveal the accusers' names until the accused have been condemned. If true, that means he does not know about me — yet.

I remove my apron and press my hair neatly under my cap, shivering with fear.

"Yes?" Juan Pablo calls when I knock on the library door.

"It is I, Maria." I straighten my skirt and try to appear composed.

"Enter."

He is seated at his father's desk, writing in a large ledger. He does not offer me a chair but waits until I am close to the desk before folding his hands and staring at me.

"You asked to see me?" I begin to tremble at his apparent coldness.

"Yes." He looks at me uncertainly. My legs turn to pudding. *Somehow he knows,* I think. *For certain — he knows!*

"Sit, Maria," he says, staring at me as if not sure where to begin. "This is not easy to say, but I will say it nevertheless." He pauses and frowns. "What happened on the way to Palos — I want to put that behind us. You were being true to what you have been raised to believe. I was too hard on you."

"No, I was wrong! I see that now. Please, forgive me!"

He holds up a hand to stop me and shakes his

head. "I also apologize for suspecting you of being an informer. Surely you must know that you are the most trusted member of our staff."

I want to scream, *What?* How can he not see my guilt?

"Since you have come to this house, you have gained the affection and respect of everyone. Mother thinks of you fondly. Angelica adores you. Though Father has little contact with you, he is a fine judge of character. He finds you kind, thoughtful, and loyal."

I feel faint. The burden of their trust is more than I can bear. I hide my face behind my hands.

"Come now," Juan Pablo says. "Do not be modest, or I will add modesty to your list of qualities."

"Please, young master," I say, unable to look at him. "Stop. I do not deserve . . ."

"I do not mean to embarrass you, Maria. Please, look at me. I have something of great importance to ask of you."

I gaze at the flowers on the desk, the large bookcase, the Moorish carpet, the painting of the Madonna and child on the wall behind him. Finally I force myself to look at Juan Pablo.

"Good," he says. He begins in a deep, low voice, leaning toward me from across the desk. "What I have to say must be between you and me only. You must speak of this to no one!"

20

a daring plan

"We must leave Spain," Juan Pablo whispers. I can tell from the ache in his voice that to say this is deeply painful for him. "I cannot imagine living anywhere else," he adds, eyes dark with sadness. "It is the place of my birth. The home of all I hold dear. I am a Spaniard first, and for Spain I would give my life." He pauses and shakes his head.

"But it is not enough to love this country. The Church demands that only true Catholics live here. First the Moors are driven out, then the Jews. And now it seems that Conversos, like my family, will be next. Do we practice any customs of our old faith?" He shrugs. "If we do, it is without intent or awareness." He takes a deep, troubled breath and adds, "We have declared our allegiance to the Catholic Church and have worshipped faithfully. We have given generously to the Church, to the King and Queen, and to the poor. But *still* we are not trusted."

My eyes remain fixed on him. My desire to comfort him, to touch his troubled face, is mixed with my shame at hearing his confidence while knowing that I am the cause of his pain.

"You know what they have done to my father."

I nod.

"If we do not leave Spain, my father will be tried and convicted and probably burned at the stake. Yet he is innocent of any crime except that of compassion for others."

My eyes never leave him.

"Which brings me to the reason I asked you here." He studies me with such attentiveness, as if he could see into my soul. His voice cracks. "We must go at once, without arousing suspicion, before the soldiers return for my father."

"Without raising suspicion?" I ask. "But the servants will guess your purpose, knowing that the Master has been accused. Someone might inform the Inquisitor." Should I warn him about Serena? But who am I to accuse another of what I am guilty of myself?

"We will tell them we are going to Palos for my wedding!"

I wince at this bitter news.

"It would give us reason to travel with more than the usual baggage. The servants will think we are bringing gifts for the bride and her family, clothing for the many festivities, my wardrobe for a permanent stay. In fact, we will be taking essentials for a new life elsewhere."

"Will the wedding take place?"

"Yes, but it will not be the festive event we would have wished."

It is the death knell of my hope. "And I? What would you have me do?"

"Pack the valuables. Serena and Margarita can pack our clothing. And again, tell no one!" He fidgets with his pen, drawing the Delgado coat of arms, then viciously crossing it out.

"If the servants ask questions, offer excuses that pertain to the wedding. We will be away for several weeks . . . there will be many festivities . . . and so on."

My head spins. Can the family reach Palos before the Inquisitors learn of their escape? Will they be able to book passage when most of the ships, laden with fleeing Jews, have already left the country?

"Where will you go?" I ask softly.

"Wherever a captain is willing to take us."

"When would we leave?"

"The day after tomorrow, God willing," Juan Pablo says. "Pray now that the soldiers do not return before then."

For a moment our eyes meet. There is between us that same warmth and affection that once was. And I see it now for what it always was for him: friendship. And the interest and light flirtation of a man who hoped to bolster my confidence — nothing more. I look away. Juan Pablo rises and walks me to the door. "Thank you, Maria," he says as we part. "Thank you for being a dear friend to my sister and a loyal servant to my family." He touches my shoulder lightly.

I want to lean toward him, to take pleasure in his touch, but stiffen instead and draw away.

When he learns of my betrayal, he will surely hate me.

21

A FRIGHTENING ENCOUNTER

It is so hard to leave. The day is warm and bright, and birds sing in the olive trees. Bougainvillea burst with color, fluttering down the white walls like tiny scarlet butterflies. I have enjoyed the happiest months of my life here.

I stand near the carriage in the courtyard, and Angelica stays close to me, watching as her mother embraces Margarita and hands her the keys to the compound "until our return." The Mistress gazes up at her large, gracious home with tears in her eyes, and I wonder if she is thinking that she may never see it again.

While Juan Pablo adjusts the bands connecting the heavily laden packhorses, Serena — with a false smile on her face — proffers a bouquet of flowers to Doña Elena. And one of the staff, with Cook beside him, carries out a huge box. She opens the lid so we can see the rich, elaborate wedding cake she baked. It smells of oranges and almonds and has a sugary frosting on top. When we exclaim, she hides her smile with a hand, then closes the box and instructs her helper to set it carefully on the carriage seat. "For the young master and his future bride," she says proudly. "Hurry home, Mistress. The house will be sad with all of you gone."

Doña Elena closes her eyes for an instant, as if she can barely control her grief. "Thank you, my dear," she says. "It is the most exquisite cake you have ever baked, and delicious too, I am sure." She fingers the cross around her neck and glances anxiously toward the men who are loading trunks onto the back of the carriage.

"I want to stay," Angelica whimpers. I press an arm around her and whisper, "Hush! Look happy, or they may think you are leaving for good!" My voice is husky from the pain I feel at this parting.

Leon comes forward. "The Master says we must leave now, Mistress. May I help you into the carriage?"

And so he does. As he lifts me aboard, he whispers, "We must talk, Maria. Soon."

And then we are on our way.

The road is open now, not crowded with Jews moving toward the seaports because the deadline for their expulsion has passed. Yet we travel more slowly than the last time because of the mules and packhorses behind our carriage. Doña Elena fingers her rosary every time she hears horses approaching. I also fear the sound, for if the Grand Inquisitor has learned of our departure, he might send soldiers after us to pluck Dr. Delgado from our midst.

The first hours are silent and tense, each of us lost in her own thoughts. I gaze out on the passing scene without seeing it, for I have such a deep feeling of unease, knowing I have no right to be here, no right to be treated as a trusted servant and friend.

For three days we travel, as before. On the fourth day, when we have left Seville, Juan Pablo trots up to the carriage to speak with Doña Elena. The tense lines on his face have eased. "Father believes we are far enough from Cáceres now, far enough to be safe. We will stop as soon as we find a good place to water the horses and rest."

Doña Elena smiles. She presses a hand to her breast and exclaims, "Thank you, dear Jesus!"

Juan Pablo waves and trots back to his position at the rear of our caravan.

A little later we stop to rest in an olive grove, as on our earlier trip. Leon leads the horses to water at a small brook, and I clear the ground of olives and lay blankets for a light repast. Yet even while we eat, our eyes are drawn to the road every time a horse and rider go by.

After our meal, Dr. Delgado and Juan Pablo speak quietly, off by themselves, perhaps about what will happen when we reach Palos. Meanwhile, Angelica, Doña Elena, and I rest in the shade. It is while we are packing to continue on our way that horses come galloping down the road we recently left.

"Eduardo!" Doña Elena cries, sitting up in alarm. "Is it . . . ? Could they be . . . ?"

"Calma, Elena," the Master says with quiet authority. "We are not the only ones who travel." Although his cheek twitches, he turns his back to the road as if the horsemen are of no concern. But as they ride closer, I feel faint when I recognize the flag of the Inquisition and the gleam of light on the soldiers' helmets. As the lead horseman turns up the slope to our small group, my palms grow damp, and my heart races. Angelica moves closer, and we reach for each other's hands.

"I will fight them, Father," Juan Pablo says, ready to pull out his sword. "They will not take you!"

"No!" Dr. Delgado holds up a hand. "We will do this my way." His face is pale, but he turns a welcoming smile on the approaching soldiers.

"In the name of King Ferdinand and Queen Isabella," the soldier in charge says, reining in his steed. "Identify yourselves!" Under the shining helmet I see a cruel face with eyes that trust no one.

"I am Don Eduardo Delgado, of Cáceres, physician to the Royal Court," the Master says, stepping forward, away from our small group. He makes a sweeping movement with one arm and adds, "My family and servants."

Should he not have given a false name? I think, alarmed. What if the soldiers carry a list with the Delgado name on it?

"Where are you going? And for what purpose?"

the soldier asks. Five other armed men, on horseback, wait attentively behind him.

"To Palos, Captain," Dr. Delgado says, with a coolness that belies what he must feel. "For the wedding of my son."

The soldier glances toward the heavily laden packhorses, and I feel dizzy, for it seems he does not believe us. He trots beside the animals and prods the leather bags hanging from their sides with his lance.

"Would you like to share in our food and drink?" Doña Elena asks softly, gesturing to the meats and cheeses still spread out on the blankets.

The soldier ignores her. "Why do you travel with so much baggage? Are you heretics, attempting to escape?"

"Certainly not!" Dr. Delgado answers, as if insulted. "We travel with many gifts for the bride and her family!"

"There is more in those pouches than gifts," the soldier says, moving toward one of the pack animals and drawing his sword. It is clear he intends to slash the leather bags that hang from the horse to prove his point. The horse whinnies and tries to shimmy away, but Leon holds tight to its reins and whispers to it.

"Wait!" I cry, running toward the mounted soldier. I glance at the Mistress, expecting her to stop me, for I am a servant and have no right to speak up. Doña Elena's eyes open wide with terror. The Master's face is flushed, and he presses a hand to his chest. My legs go weak as the soldier finally gazes down at me.

"Excuse me, kind sir," I say. "Though I am a lowly servant, please hear me out. We *are* going to a wedding, as Dr. Delgado says!" I gasp, suddenly out of breath. The soldier's lips are thin, twisted into a derisive smile. There is a scar on his left cheek. I sense he has little patience left, and I am of no importance to him. My heart pounds as I try once more. "I can prove it!"

"How?" he asks.

"I have packed much of what the Delgados carry. In the carriage, sir, there is a large box. Inside is the wedding cake. And . . . and . . ." I run to the horse that Leon is holding and point to one of the packs. "I can open this, if you wish. Inside are the dresses the Mistress and her daughter will wear for the wedding!" I run to the next horse. "And in this bag are silver candlesticks to give to the bride's parents! Shall I open it and show you?"

The soldier regards me quizzically, not sure whether to believe a servant, and does not answer. He turns and weaves his horse in and out of our camp, studying each pack animal and each of us as if he could tell by some sign whether we are telling the truth. Leon and I exchange terrified glances, and we follow his movements as anxiously as we would the course of a poisonous snake. At last the Captain stops near the coach and peers inside to see if there is indeed a large box. He dismounts, climbs into the carriage, and opens the lid. "Ahh," he exclaims when he sees the cake. He withdraws a knife from its scabbard and cuts a square, plugging the cake into his mouth. Crumbs fall from his lips. "Ahh," he says again.

With another square of cake in hand, he rides up to Dr. Delgado and says, no longer belligerent, "You understand, Sir, that we have been ordered to examine every caravan on the road. There are many Conversos the Grand Inquisitor would like to question. Those who try to leave are especially suspect, for why would they go if they have nothing to hide?"

"Why indeed?" the Master asks, leaning heavily on Doña Elena. "Is there anything more we can do for you?"

"No, Sir."

"Then I commend you on your diligence, Captain, and I will say good day."

The soldier nods to Juan Pablo. "And to you, Sir, the very best of luck on your forthcoming marriage." He signals the soldiers waiting nearby and trots back to the road.

I am light-headed with relief. Angelica runs to my side and hugs me. "You were wonderful!" she exclaims.

"Yes, child," Doña Elena says. "I thought for certain we would be taken into custody."

"Good thinking there, girl," the Master says, helped onto his horse by Leon.

Juan Pablo smiles at me, a look that is both admiring and affectionate. My face burns with self-consciousness. "It was nothing," I murmur. "Nada." I kneel to wrap up the last of the food to take to the coach, trying to hide my pleasure. I want to skip and dance and run in a crazy circle. Perhaps I have done one small thing to right my terrible wrong.

22

COLD WELCOME

One of the household must have gone ahead to alert the Perreiras, for they show no surprise at our arrival. Instead of the joyous greetings of our first visit, the embraces are quick and restrained. Bowing to Catherine, Juan Pablo withdraws almost immediately to stand by his father.

I think, perhaps wrongly, that the Perreiras are not pleased to see us, that they seem wary and anxious. Could they fear that if the Inquisitors learn the Delgados are with them that they too, might become suspects?

"Thank you, dear friend, for receiving us on such short notice," Dr. Delgado says to Catherine's father. "We are weary, and most grateful, for we have traveled hard."

"You are always welcome," Señor Perreira says, though his manner is unconvincing. "My servants will help unload your things. Come inside and rest. Then we shall talk."

The families seem like strangers to each other. They move toward the castle in separate groups — not like the last visit, when they walked together, chattering like happy birds.

"What is wrong, Mama?" Angelica whispers as we cross the castle courtyard. "Are the Perreiras not happy to see us?"

"Of course they are, my dear. It is just that — we are all very tired," Doña Elena replies.

"May Maria sleep with me tonight, please?" she pleads.

"If you wish." The Mistress turns to me. "I do not know how long we will stay. Do not unpack everything, Maria." She gives me a knowing look.

"The wedding clothes, Mistress?"

"Not just yet. We shall see."

Does she mean that the wedding might not take place after all? Such news gives me pleasure for a moment. Is there still hope? Foolish thought. I know now that Juan Pablo never loved me as I dared imagine. And that he and Catherine are suited to each other. If they do not marry, how sad it would be. Another thorn in my heart.

The last time we were in Palos, I stayed with the servants, rarely within the castle rooms where the Delgados and Perreiras dwelled. Never privy to their conversations or plans unless told to join Angelica. Now, because the mood is so different, I share a bedchamber with Angelica. We are together almost constantly.

"Come with me," she beckons after dinner the first evening. "The others will be talking about the wedding. I know where to hide so we can listen."

"But — " I start to object, then stop myself. I know it is not proper to listen, uninvited, to others. But I am as curious as she.

She knows the interior passageways of the castle as well as the halls of her own home. She has hidden in wardrobes, under stairs, behind doors — to overhear adult secrets.

Carrying candles, we tread down long corridors dimly lit by candles in wall sconces. It is so dank in some places that the walls weep. The air smells of mildew and the droppings of mice. I think of the prison where they took Dr. Delgado and wonder if it smelled like this.

We arrive, finally, in an anteroom near the stone stairway, next to a closed double door. Angelica presses a finger to her lips and an ear to the wood, then frowns. "Follow me. I know a better place to listen."

Shielding her candle, she flies down another hall, with me behind, and enters the kitchen. Slowing to a stride, Angelica smiles at the cooks and moves past them through more rooms as if she has every right to do so. Finally we arrive at a door that she opens a crack. It is the back entrance to the great room where the two families are meeting. I am breathless for fear of being caught.

But Angelica merely slides to the floor and moves close to the opening in the door, motioning me to do the same. We sit and watch and listen.

The families are seated on facing chairs. Their voices echo in the room.

"If you had given us more notice," Señor Perreira says, "we could have arranged all you expect. But the wedding was not to be until — "

Dr. Delgado interrupts. "We had no choice. We *have* no choice. We must leave Spain as soon as possible. If the marriage is to take place, it must be immediately."

"May I speak, please?" Señora Perreira asks.

"What is it, my dear?" her husband answers.

Señora Perreira's voice is strident. "The understanding was that after the marriage, Juan Pablo would remain in Palos so that Catherine would be close by. Now you speak of leaving Spain? Going to some distant land? And taking our daughter!"

"Do you not realize," the Master asks with irritation, "that no one of Jewish ancestry — not even a Converso — is now safe?"

Señor Perreira scoffs. "Eduardo! What are you saying? Surely you must know our standing in the court. Would the King have given me this castle if he doubted my loyalty to Church and Crown?"

"Did I think *my* loyalty would be questioned? That *I* would be accused of heresy?" Dr. Delgado, asks, nearly choking on the words. Through the crack in the door I see that his face has turned a deep red. He begins to cough violently, clutching his chest.

"Eduardo!" Doña Elena cries in alarm.

Juan Pablo rushes to his father's side.

Angelica gasps and squeezes my arm. I want so much to help and feel so useless.

"You are ill!" Señor Perreira rises and rings for a servant.

The Master recovers enough to shake his head. "It is nothing. The strain. A moment . . ."

With one hand on his father's shoulder, Juan Pablo takes over. "My father is charged with helping a dear friend, a Jew, to leave Spain!" he says.

Is this what Dr. Delgado is accused of? Could it be that I am not the cause of all their troubles? I cannot even fathom what it means.

Juan Pablo goes on, his voice rising with passion. "A Jew! A man he loved and respected but by law was forbidden to speak to or help. Would you have done otherwise? Would you not hope someone would help *you* if the positions were reversed?"

"I have no commerce with Jews," Señor Perreira says, "no matter what the circumstances!"

"Dear friend!" Dr. Delgado exclaims, once more in control of himself. "And do you have commerce with those who *aid* Jews?"

Señor Perreira flushes with embarrassment and drops his voice. "Let us not quarrel, Eduardo. You are safe here with my family. If you are intent upon leaving Spain, I will do everything possible to help you."

"And the wedding?" Doña Elena asks.

"I do not want to lose my daughter!" There is a catch in Señora Perreira's voice. "Perhaps . . . if Juan Pablo remains?"

Doña Elena stiffens but does not reply.

"We are very tired." The Master's tone is as sad and as weary as he looks. "Let us speak of this again tomorrow." Juan Pablo helps him to his feet.

"Hurry!" Angelica whispers. "We must not be seen." She closes the door quietly. Then, clutching our candles, we race back through the maze of corridors and rooms to her bedchamber.

There is so much anxiety and strain here. And though the doctor has been accused for other reasons than what I confided to Fra Adolfo, I am sure my words contributed to his fate.

But I cannot afford to focus on my guilt. Dr. Delgado must find passage for his family quickly. They are not welcome in this house, and the Inquisitors will be searching for him soon, if not already. I must help. But how?

23

Betrayed

Once we are safely back in our room, Angelica no longer whispers. "I hate it here!" she cries, stomping back and forth. "They do not want us! And Catherine's mother is wicked! She will not let her marry Juan Pablo unless he stays in Palos!"

"Oh, Angelica! How would you feel if your only daughter went so far away you might never see her again?" I ask.

She tosses her curls angrily. "I do not care about her feelings! I care about *ours!* Mama is frightened. Do you see how she prays all the time? Juan Pablo hardly speaks. And tomorrow, though he is ill, Papa will look for a ship that will take us away. What if he cannot find one?" Her eyes fill with tears.

"He will find a ship," I say with a certainty I do not feel. "He has money. He is not like the Jews, who had little to offer for passage."

"And Maria!" she rushes on, not seeming to hear a word I say. Her voice tightens. "What will become of *you*? Where will *you* go?" She throws her arms around me. "How will I manage without you? You are my dearest friend!"

We hold each other close and cry in each other's arms.

There are no answers to these questions.

The next day Leon accompanies Dr. Delgado and Juan Pablo to the docks. The Mistress, Angelica, and I pass the hours in the garden. It is a hot, sleepy day. Bees buzz among the flowers, and the air is heavy with the scent of roses.

We sit on a bench in the only shade. Doña Elena struggles to concentrate on her embroidery, but every few minutes she puts down her work, sighs, and stares off into the distance. Angelica and I try to play chess, but neither of us can focus on the game. We whisper instead about Catherine, wondering why she avoids us and what she is thinking. Neither she nor her mother seek our company.

At last the men return. Leon hurries away to see to the horses. I search Dr. Delgado's face as he and Juan Pablo stride directly to Doña Elena. He looks tense and grim.

"It is arranged," the Master says in a flat voice. He fans his face with his wide-brimmed hat. "I told you not to fear. It was not easy, for there are few ships in port since the Jews left. But I have found a captain who will take us."

Angelica lets out a happy squeal, and I clap my hands.

"Take us — where?" Doña Elena asks.

"The Ottoman Empire."

Doña Elena clutches her cross. She does not look pleased. "The Ottoman Empire?"

"That is where his ship is going."

"But we do not know the language! It is so — uncivilized! It is a Muslim land — and we are Catholic!"

"Mother," Juan Pablo says, close to exasperation. "We are leaving Spain because of religion, and you question the faith of the land that would accept us?"

Doña Elena frowns.

"Do not fear, dear Elena," the Master says gently. "We will survive this nightmare. They start loading our baggage tonight, and the ship leaves the day after tomorrow."

Juan Pablo kneels before his mother and takes her hands. "Be glad, Mother. This captain is taking a chance. The harbor is full of soldiers looking for Jews who did not leave by the expulsion date."

"Jews, perhaps, but certainly not for us?" she asks, suddenly alarmed.

"No!" the Master replies sharply. "They would not be looking for us!"

I think he lies, that he believes otherwise but does not wish to alarm the Mistress.

I feel uncomfortable witnessing this exchange, and move back into the shadows. With all this talk of leaving, I have heard nothing about what is to become of me.

"What about the wedding?" Angelica asks. "And what about Maria? Will she go with us?"

The Master turns to his daughter, and his face softens. "The marriage is still uncertain, sweet angel." He sighs and nods to me. "And as for Maria . . . I will see to it that she has sufficient income to live on until she finds a new position."

"But Papa!" Angelica protests. "I want Maria to come too!"

"Stop, Angelica! Do not argue. I have decided."

I look on guiltily and murmur thanks, though I wish the Master had said that I might go with them.

How could I ever have wanted to hurt these people? Though I do penance, shame hangs heavily on me. Still, I feel less burdened now that I know they will soon be safely away.

In the morning I learn that the wedding will take place after all. A priest has agreed to preside on short notice. Only a few close friends will attend. The families have reached a compromise. Now, Juan Pablo and Catherine will go with the Delgados, but each year they will return to Spain, if possible, to visit the Perreiras.

Preparations for the marriage should be joyful, but I feel no joy in those around me. Everything must be done in a day. Right after the festivities the Delgados are to leave. It is too sudden; neither family seems ready for it. Their eyes show fear and uncertainty. Señora Perreira is especially on edge. She barks orders at the servants who decorate the banquet hall and criticizes the flower arrangements and the way the tables are set for the dinner to follow the wedding. When Catherine embraces her mother, Señora Perreira sobs and thrusts her away.

I spend much of the final morning pressing the satin-and-lace gowns that Angelica and Doña Elena will wear, and setting out gifts for Catherine and her family. Yesterday I repacked the trunks for shipboard. Almost all of the clothes had to be sent on ahead. The family will carry the valuables on board, Doña Elena told me.

Even though I am busy helping Angelica and Doña Elena, thoughts of my own future keep intruding. Today, Juan Pablo will wed. Though I have come to accept the rightness of his union with Catherine, it still pains me. And tomorrow, if all goes as planned, the family I have come to love will be gone. I will be on my own. I shiver at the prospect.

While the wedding party is inside the chapel, I sit on a bench outside with Leon. He is dressed in a clean white shirt and dark trousers and looks quite handsome. I wear my going-to-church dress of soft blue wool. We were not invited to the ceremony and wait for it to end, awkward with each other in the new circumstances.

"Where is Roberto?" I ask.

"The Master sent him to the docks to check on the ship."

"Mistress Catherine looked so beautiful," I say, trying to continue the conversation.

"As *you* will on *your* wedding day." Leon takes my hand and holds it firmly.

What is he doing? My heart suddenly pounds in my ears. How dare he be so familiar? Do I want this? Do I like it? I do not know.

"What will you do when they leave?" I ask, staring straight ahead, uncertain whether to leave my hand in his or withdraw it.

"The Master has promised me money. I will open my own stable. I am good with horses. And you?"

"Perhaps I could work for the Perreiras."

"What? Is that what you would do?" He squeezes my hand for emphasis. "Shame! You can read! You play a musical instrument! Have you no higher goals than working again as a servant?"

I pull my hand from his. Who is he to question my plans? What choices have I other than being a servant? Yet his question sets me thinking. Perhaps there *are* other options, though what they are I do not know. The freedom to choose is new, and I am not yet comfortable with it.

"You could even marry me," he says lightly, glancing quickly in my direction. "You could teach our children to read." He chuckles.

Is he joking? Marriage? Children? I gape, too surprised to know how to answer. Luckily, at this moment, Roberto comes hobbling toward us.

He is wild-eyed and out of breath and bends over before us, hands on his knees. He points to the chapel door. "Not out yet?"

"Soon," I say. "Is something wrong?"

"It is too terrible, too terrible!" he mutters, panting and shaking his head.

"Roberto, what is it? Tell us!" Leon commands, helping the old man to a seat. He pulls a flask from his pocket and holds it out.

Roberto takes a long, deep drink and wipes his sweating face and neck with a rag.

"Roberto!" Leon insists. "Tell us at once!"

"The ship," he finally says, ". . . that Dr. Delgado booked passage on. . ." He pauses to catch his breath.

"Yes?" Leon demands.

"Gone! Sailed away! With all the Delgados' goods! With everything we loaded last night!" His panting gives way to moaning. "The captain insisted the Master pay in advance. I do not know how much, but many maravedis!" The horror of what he is saying is reflected in his wide-eyed stare.

"Sailed? Impossible!" Leon barks.

"I saw it for myself!" Roberto wails. "It was just a speck, far out to sea. At first I thought my eyes were deceiving me. Thought maybe the captain might have changed berths. But it was true. She sailed at dawn!"

What terrible news. I cannot believe it. "Why? Why would the captain not wait?" My voice shakes.

Behind the chapel doors come sounds of movement. The ceremony must be over.

"Because of the soldiers," Roberto answers. "Sailors told me the captain got frightened when they said they were looking for a Converso, a man from Cáceres by the name of Delgado!"

"Dios mio!" I whisper, pressing my hands to my face. "Leon! They know he is in Palos. What will the Master do now?"

24

a su∂∂en inspiration

The doors open, and Juan Pablo and Catherine emerge, hand in hand. Catherine smiles as she passes. Juan Pablo is solemn, though he does not yet know the terrible news.

"Felicidades," I say, and curtsy.

Next come the Perreiras. Señor Perreira seems flustered, and his wife weeps openly. The Delgados follow, with Doña Elena clutching her husband's arm and Angelica trailing behind them, carrying a bouquet of blue and white flowers. The few guests and the priest come last.

As Leon closes the heavy chapel doors, Roberto limps after Dr. Delgado. "Master," he says urgently, "I would speak with you for a moment."

Dr. Delgado hesitates, then nods.

"Forgive me, my dear," he tells Doña Elena. "Go with Angelica and Maria to the dining hall. I will join you presently."

I wish I could stay, but women are not welcome to hear or take part in men's conversation. I obediently follow the others down the torch-lit hall nearby.

"I wonder what Roberto wants," Doña Elena muses. I glance back frequently to where Roberto, Dr. Delgado, and Leon now huddle. Angelica chatters happily about the wedding ceremony, oblivious to my distraction.

The three men arrive at the wedding banquet quite late. The great hall, which could seat hundreds, echoes with the voices of fewer than twenty servants and perhaps as many guests. I sit stiffly with the Perreiras' servants, sickened by their vulgar jokes and laughter and close to tears with worry.

Leon slides into a seat beside me, closes his eyes, and shakes his head. Across the way Dr. Delgado joins Doña Elena at the head table. He looks grim, drained of color. Roberto's news has struck him hard. What will he do now?

Doña Elena leans toward him, asking, I imagine, what Roberto had to say. He pats her shoulder and turns to the Perreiras, as if all is well.

"He will give himself up," Leon states flatly, leaning toward me.

"What?" I stare at him in disbelief.

"With the soldiers so close after him, he endangers everyone — his family, you, me, the Perreiras. He says no sea captain will chance taking the family now that it is known he is wanted."

A servant carries a meat-laden platter to our table. There is a hum of approval. Many hands greedily reach for the moist hunks of lamb and chicken. The smell nauseates me.

"*Someone* will take them," I whisper. "They *must!*"

Leon shakes his head. He lifts half a chicken onto his plate. "Yesterday Dr. Delgado boarded every ship in the harbor. He pleaded, offered great sums of money. . . . One captain said that he would do it but that his ship would not be seaworthy for at least two weeks. Only the captain of *El Oceano* agreed — and now he is gone."

I watch Juan Pablo across the way. He offers Catherine a sip from his wine cup and tenderly touches her copper hair. Angelica laughs and claps her hands. They are happy. They do not know.

I have no appetite for food or celebration. It seems so hopeless. Can I do anything to help?

Leon passes a platter of food to me. I turn my face away.

"Starving will not help them," he says gently, serving me a chicken leg.

"Neither will feasting!" Food makes me think suddenly of Uncle Francisco, a man of great girth who loved to eat more than he loved women. "Leon!" I cry, excited at the thought. *"My uncle!"*

He tears a chunk of chicken from the bone, chews it noisily, and waits for me to explain.

"Could he possibly be in Palos by now?"

He nods and wipes away the meat juices that have

dripped down his chin. "I saw the ship — *La Gran Esperanza* — but was told that many of the crew have been at sea a long time and are down with the sailor's sickness. The captain is a Francisco Sanchez — your uncle, perhaps. He was not aboard the ship at the time we inquired, so we could not speak with him."

"Take me to the ship." I tug at his shirt. "Maybe — if *I* talk with him — "

"Now?" Leon reaches for a chunk of lamb.

"Now! Is filling our bellies more important than helping the Delgados?" I rise, and in doing so catch Juan Pablo's attention. For an instant our eyes lock, and my heart beats faster. "One of the Delgados should be with us. Ask Juan Pablo if he will come."

I watch as Leon crosses the dining hall to the head table. He leans close to Juan Pablo and whispers to him. Juan Pablo stands, excuses himself with a frozen smile, and follows Leon from the room.

I join the two outside the dining hall. Leon tells Juan Pablo what Roberto has discovered, then explains that his father intends to surrender to the Inquisitors now that there is no hope to leave Spain.

"Why did he not tell me? I am his son!" he cries.

"No doubt he did not want to spoil your wedding," I say.

Juan Pablo covers his face with his hands and shakes his head in despair. "We are lost. I see no way to escape if the Inquisition knows Father is here."

"You must not give up!" I protest. "There is yet a

chance! I have an uncle, a sea captain. We think he is in Palos. Perhaps, because I am his niece, he would take you!"

Juan Pablo looks from me to Leon and back, as if unable to absorb all we have said.

"Need we ask your father's permission first?" I say, anxious to be on our way. "And will you come with us?"

"Of course I will! Father need not be told. Why raise his hopes, only to have them dashed?"

We hurry to the stables, where the grooms quickly saddle two horses, one for Juan Pablo and the other to carry Leon and me.

As we trot down the hill toward the road to Palos, Juan Pablo leads the way. I sit behind Leon, holding him around the waist as I once did Juan Pablo. But it is not the same, for this time my heart pounds with uncertainty and fear, not desire.

I pray Captain Francisco Sanchez *is* my uncle. Will I even recognize him? I have not seen him in five years. I remember a big man as soft as a pillow, a jovial giant who made my mother laugh. Will he recognize me? Will he be put off because I have come begging?

Mama said Uncle was a cautious man, so why should he risk imprisonment for helping a man wanted by the Inquisition?

These questions tumble through my head as we approach the harbor, and I am suddenly terrified at the prospect of seeing this stranger, my uncle, again.

25

la gran esperanza

Palos is not as it was weeks ago when the streets and shops swelled with people, when ships sailed each day, loaded with the desperate Jews. It is quiet now, cleaner and less odorous, with few vessels in the harbor, few sailors about, and fewer people on the streets. Which makes the soldiers of the Inquisition even more visible.

As we approach *La Gran Esperanza*, three soldiers pause in their patrol of the harbor and come forward, asking for identification. My legs tremble. Now we are undone.

"Henrique!" Leon greets one of them heartily. "You must remember me! The alehouse last night?"

The soldier's eyes narrow as he examines Leon. "Ah, yes! The fellow who knows horses so well! What are you doing with a young lady, boarding that boat with the sick ones?"

I stiffen, but force a smile.

"The captain is her uncle! She has not seen him in a long time," Leon answers.

Juan Pablo links an arm through mine. "Dare we let a good young lady find her way alone in a town roaring with ill-mannered, lusty sailors?"

"And *soldiers*," Leon adds, winking.

The men laugh. "Go on, go on!" Henrique says. "We are not all bad!"

I let out the breath I held these last moments and climb aboard *La Gran Esperanza*. It is a wooden vessel, smaller than Columbus's *Santa Maria*. It looks like it has seen many years at sea and is not well cared for. The sails need mending. The brass fittings need polishing. The deck needs sanding and refinishing. But what do I know of sailing vessels and their seaworthiness?

Only a few sailors are tending to the ship. Most of the crew seem listless. Many lie about on the deck.

"We are here to speak with Captain Francisco Sanchez," Leon says to a sailor who rises to question us. The man is almost toothless, and when he speaks, I see that his gums are swollen and red, and I smell a foul stench coming from his mouth. Is it from the sickness Leon spoke of?

"This is Maria Sanchez, his niece," Leon adds.

I offer a shy smile and silently pray that I am indeed what Leon claims.

Leon whistles softly. Juan Pablo stares ahead to the stairway where the sailor disappeared. I wait, silent, dry-mouthed with anxiety.

"Maria? Maria Sanchez? My sister's daughter? Is that you, my dear?"

Coming toward me is this great hulk of a man. It *is* my uncle! His beard is gray now, and his skin darker than I remember, but his eyes have the same sparkling warmth. He holds out his enormous arms, the size of tree trunks, to embrace me.

"Uncle!" I cry, suddenly wailing in big, gulping sobs. I run hungrily into those arms.

"Ah, little one," he croons, stroking my face, as if no time has passed since last we met. His voice breaks. "What are you doing here? How is my sister, and your father?" He does not ask about Carlos, who was born after he left. "Come into my cabin," he says, with a sweeping gesture that includes Leon and Juan Pablo. "We will talk."

We sit in the small, dark cabin, my uncle's home at sea, in chairs surrounding a table crowded with maps. The boat rocks and creaks as the water laps at its sides. I forget about Juan Pablo and Leon, for my eyes and heart are linked only to my uncle. It is so good to tell him about the years since he visited. I do not even cry when I speak of the deaths of Mama and Papa and little Carlos, and how I came to live with the Delgados. Nor do I cry when I talk about the terrible captain who sailed away with all the Delgados' hopes. It is a long story, and my uncle listens attentively, his eyes never leaving my face.

"I know the captain you speak of," he says. "I have

had dealings with him. He is a thief, a rogue, a man without honor."

At last I come to the reason for my visit. My voice quavers. "Can you help them, Uncle?" I ask. "I know it is dangerous because the soldiers are looking for Dr. Delgado. Yes, he is a Converso, but he has done no harm. He is a good man, with a good family. Can they sail with you?"

When I see the doubt, the sudden tightness of my uncle's jaw, I fear all is lost. I remember that he is a cautious man and not likely to undertake such risk for strangers. In desperation I cry out, unheeding that Juan Pablo and Leon will hear: "It may be because of *me* that they are in danger! Uncle, listen! I was hurt and jealous and told the priest things I should not have said. It may be because of me that Dr. Delgado is wanted!"

I burst out crying and sob as if there is no end to tears. "There, there," my uncle clucks. He hands me a handkerchief to dry my tears. Ashamed, but glad at last to have unburdened my heart, I look up. Juan Pablo is glaring at me, aghast.

"My crew is ill," Uncle Francisco explains, not unkindly. "Even if I would agree, I could not promise when they would be well enough to sail."

"Dr. Delgado can pay well. You could hire a new crew," Leon suggests.

"My father is a doctor!" Juan Pablo exclaims. "And I too am skilled. Perhaps we can cure your sailors' sickness!"

My uncle raises a hand to stop them. "Impossible. It is not just my crew. You say the soldiers of the Inquisition are already searching for your father." He looks directly at Juan Pablo. "And he would bring with him his wife and daughter, and you and your bride. That many people boarding a ship would be suspicious. No. I sympathize, but I want no trouble."

"We could board at night!" Juan Pablo argues.

"Yes!" Leon takes up the argument. "The soldiers are often in the alehouse then. I know some of them. I could see they have much to drink, for I would pay for their ale and toast their success in catching infidels!"

Uncle Francisco scratches his head. "That is all very well, but someone might notice and report to the authorities. No, too risky."

I twist my hands in anguish, struggling to find an answer to his objection.

"Disguise!" I cry at last. "We could dress the Master as a sailor! Juan Pablo, too. Have them board with their duffels, as if they belong to the ship." I stare wide-eyed at my uncle, trying to fathom if there is hope, silently willing him to do what I ask.

He rubs his rough beard, considering. "And the women? Would you dress them as sailors, too?"

I shake my head. "When Doña Elena arrives, you greet her as if she is your dear wife, come to sail with you. Catherine and Angelica could embrace you as your daughters!"

My uncle lets out a loud guffaw and pats my leg so

hard I wince. "Clever girl. You have thought of every-thing!"

"Then will you? Please, Uncle Francisco, I beg you. For Mama and Papa and baby Carlos? For me? Please!"

"Not for those reasons, child, but perhaps — should I so decide — because despots must be stopped. I have known Catholics, and I have known Jews and Moors. To me it does not matter what God they worship, only that they are honest and good. Punishing people because of their religious beliefs makes no sense."

I nod. My own experience has taught me this.

He chuckles. "To save the Delgados from the Inquisition would be a small satisfaction."

I leap from my chair and run behind him to hug his huge bulk from the back. I nuzzle my face against his wiry hair and murmur, "Thank you — oh, thank you dear uncle! I prayed you would help!"

"Maria, my dear," he chides, shrugging away from my embrace, "I did not say I *would*. I only said I would *think* about it. I promise nothing."

26

last hope

On the ride back to the castle, I am jubilant — perhaps without good cause — wanting to believe that my uncle will give the Delgados safe passage from Spain. But I am uneasy too. Leon and Juan Pablo now know the truth: I betrayed the family.

I secretly watch Juan Pablo as we trot back, but cannot read his thoughts. Can he possibly like or respect me now?

We say little until we reach the castle grounds and dismount.

"I must speak with my father," Juan Pablo says to Leon. "Maria, come with me."

We hasten through the long halls of the castle. The only sound is that of Juan Pablo's boots slapping the stone floors, a slap of disapproval.

I run along beside him, trying to keep up with his

long strides. "Please," I beg, my voice breaking. "Let me explain!"

Juan Pablo stops abruptly and turns to me, his face dark with rage. "My father's being accused is not all your fault. But why did you betray us? Why?"

I could blame my betrayal on Fra Adolfo. But that would be too easy. In truth, I had a choice. I did not have to yield to his pressure. I take a deep breath and say, "I wish I could say I had a good reason, but then I would be lying."

Juan Pablo's eyes burn with anger.

"I am ashamed to admit that I was . . . envious. I wanted more than I had a right to. I wanted your family's respect and attention, and thought they had withdrawn them. I wanted . . . your affection." My cheeks flame with embarrassment, but I hold Juan Pablo's gaze until he looks away.

"Please forgive me," I whisper. "I went to Fra Adolfo to take back what I said, but he would not see me." I hear tears in my voice.

When Juan Pablo looks back at me, I see disappointment in his face — and perhaps acceptance. He starts back down the hall.

"Will you tell the others?" I ask, hurrying after him, horrified at that possibility.

"What good would it do? No. You are trying to make amends. For that I am grateful. We all are. Now we must look at our choices."

When we reach the great hall, the banquet is over; servants are clearing the tables. They direct us to a nearby sitting room where the families have gathered.

Dr. Delgado must have revealed the loss of the ship and his plan to surrender, for even before we reach the room, we hear loud voices.

Señor Perreira shouts, "Enough of this caterwauling! It is no way to solve our problems!"

Catherine's strained voice begs, "Mama! Por favor! We are one family now. I too am a Delgado. We must seek solutions together!"

As we enter, Señora Perreira pulls away from her daughter's touch. She points at her husband. "They could arrest you, too! All of us! The Inquisition says he is a *criminal!*"

"A criminal? How dare you call my husband a criminal!" Doña Elena screams.

Angelica wails, "If they take Papa, they will torture him! They will tie him up and burn him!"

"Enough!" the Master bellows. "Elena, Angelica — come! We will leave immediately for home."

Juan Pablo pauses only long enough to hear this last exchange, then strides forward with me close behind. "Wait, Father!" he calls, extending a hand to restrain his father.

"Juan Pablo! At last you are back! Where were you?" the Master demands.

"We may have found a captain who will take us to Portugal!"

"What?" Dr. Delgado cries in disbelief.

I can hardly breathe, fearful that Juan Pablo will tell them what I confessed to him. But instead he reaches back and pulls me in front of him. "Tell them, Maria. About your uncle. You are the one who made this possible."

Each day we wait with anxious impatience for word from Uncle Francisco. Juan Pablo leaves early every morning and rides to the docks to speak with my uncle. To help time pass, Angelica, Catherine, and I play games without enthusiasm and read aloud to each other, or do needlepoint, but always with an ear tuned to the road for Juan Pablo's return with news. But day follows day with no encouraging word.

I try to bolster hope by repeating my uncle's tirade against despots. How he claimed saving the Delgados from the Inquisition would give him special satisfaction.

But if that is so — why does he not act?

"He is a stubborn man, Maria's uncle, stubborn and cautious, as Maria told us," Juan Pablo explains, after a day in Palos. To be less conspicuous, he has begun dressing like a sailor. Though he is speaking to his family, he looks my way from time to time, including me.

"Did you tell Captain Sanchez what may cure his crew?" Dr. Delgado asks. He looks old these days — shrunken, thinner, no longer the robust master I first came to know.

"I told him," Juan Pablo says, "that eating mostly

salt pork and beans and no fresh vegetables or fruit on long voyages might cause the illness from which the sailors suffer."

"And?"

"He scoffed — and advised you not to tell others of this *cure* or your status as physician will be questioned. Still, he said he might take cabbages on the next voyage, for they store well." Juan Pablo's mouth curls into a slight smile. "If his crew consumed them, he joked, he would not need sails for the *wind* the men would produce."

Dr. Delgado does not smile. "I am pleased he found my suggestion amusing. But has he still no word about taking us?"

"None."

"I cannot even leave the castle for fear of being apprehended. How long must we wait?"

Uncle Francisco is our only hope. What *is* taking so long? I am certain he will not turn me down. And yet, with each day that passes without a decision, it becomes harder to remain sure. Even Juan Pablo appears to lose hope. He says that he has run out of pleas and arguments and that it is not a matter of money to Uncle Francisco, but of whether he will risk his ship and his career.

Whenever I see soldiers galloping on the road below the castle, I think they must be coming here, and I stiffen until they pass. I wonder why they have not stormed the castle to take Dr. Delgado. Are their orders to capture him only if he tries to leave Spanish soil?

As the days wear on, our earlier jubilation turns to hopelessness and finally acceptance. "The captain's silence is his answer," Dr. Delgado announces. "It is time to return to Cáceres and face whatever comes."

There is much moaning and objection, but there seems no other choice, and his word is law. As frightening as the prospect of returning is, I think we are all ready to leave. Waiting has put everyone on edge. The Perreiras are polite but distant, as if each day the Delgados stay they are less welcome.

Suddenly, on the morning we are packed for our journey home, a messenger arrives with news.

Dr. Delgado opens the sealed envelope with trembling fingers and reads the message first to himself, then to us. "Crew's health improving on diet you prescribed. Board by midnight. Bring little. We sail at first light tomorrow. Francisco Sanchez."

"Oh, Papa!" Angelica cries, hugging her father happily.

"Thank you, heavenly Father!" Catherine whispers.

Doña Elena's face flushes. "Bring little? We have so little left after that thief of a sea captain made off with our things. Are we to leave behind all Catherine's beautiful clothes, her linens, the wedding gifts, not to mention our valuables — the paintings, the jewelry?"

"My dear," Dr. Delgado says impatiently. "You

worry about 'things' at a time like this? Things can be replaced. What we still have is each other and now — the promise of a future!"

I watch these people as if from afar. This news, which I have hoped for with every breath I draw, now means the breaking of the bond I have with them.

I love so much what I am about to lose — Angelica, whose curiosity and eagerness for every new experience has taught me to be more adventurous; steadfast but timid Doña Elena, who lacks the courage of her husband; even gentle Catherine, though I do not know her well. And of course, Juan Pablo. My throat tightens with tears at the thought that after tonight I shall never see him or them again.

All afternoon we consider what to take and what to leave, for Dr. Delgado has limited Doña Elena to two satchels. He and Juan Pablo will carry one canvas bag each. Angelica insists on taking a roll of my drawings, though it takes up much space in her satchel. Doña Elena fusses over which valuables and keepsakes to take and finally collapses in tears with indecision.

When we have finally finished packing, Angelica flings her arms around me and buries her head in my shoulder. "Maria! The soldiers will be watching who leaves the castle. What if they arrest Papa? We cannot leave without him! Oh, I am so frightened!"

"Shhh, dear angel," I croon. "Shhh." I cannot find words to allay her fears, for they are my fears, too.

27

at first light

When we are ready to leave the castle grounds, it is dark but for a sliver of moon in the sky. In this we are fortunate. Dr. Delgado and Juan Pablo left earlier, with Leon accompanying them to bring back the horses. I worry that the soldiers of the Inquisition might stop and question them. Neither father nor son could pass as ordinary sailors. Their speech would surely betray them. I worry, too, how they will board *La Gran Esperanza* when it is said the soldiers are now checking everyone more closely. I say the same prayers for them over and over. But the question lingers: Will my plan work?

In the last minutes before we leave, the Perreira family gathers for good-byes. Señora Perreira sobs and clings to Catherine, begging her to change her mind, to stay. Her husband stands by, stiff and worried, eyes also fixed upon Catherine. Though I am not much fond of the Perreiras, my heart goes out to them, for their grief is real and deep. I dare not think about the next few hours, for soon I will suffer the same pain of parting.

We are silent as Roberto drives us to the port in the carriage. Will there be trouble when the women try to board? Can I bear to be without Doña Elena and Angelica? My stomach churns, and I fight back tears.

Doña Elena stares out the window into the darkness, fingering her cross, her mouth moving, surely, in prayer. Catherine dabs at her eyes. Angelica clings to me like a child to her mother.

A short distance from my uncle's ship, Roberto hands us down from the carriage. We embrace, too quickly, and turn to the quay. Torches light the ship and the ladder hanging from its deck. On the quay a number of unruly sailors crowd together, drinking, laughing, and singing. Soldiers on horseback move in and out of the raucous throng, perhaps trying to disperse the merrymakers. Or searching for infidels? It is hard to tell from this distance. We draw closer. I will not leave Doña Elena and Angelica until they are safely in my uncle's charge.

"How will we ever get past those drunkards?" Doña Elena asks, voice trembling.

"Do not worry, Mistress," Roberto assures her. "Captain Sanchez has arranged this diversion. See! There he is, watching for you. Ah. Here he comes now!"

Indeed, upon our approach my uncle starts down

the ladder. It sways from his great weight. He holds on with one hand and salutes us with the other.

Doña Elena stiffens but moves forward.

"Remember," I whisper, "he is your husband, and you have not seen him in months! Remember, Angelica and Catherine! You are his daughters."

The sailors seem to know where we are going and make a path for us, blocking the soldiers from drawing near.

"Dear lady, dear wife!" Uncle Francisco bellows, taking Doña Elena's hand and pressing it to his lips. "Daughters! My dears! How you have grown!"

I wait beside them, left out of their drama, awaiting a signal about what to do next. I had imagined a moment before parting when Angelica and I could say good-bye properly. When I might thank Doña Elena for my happy days in her home. All that should have been done at the castle, I realize now.

Angelica waves back to me as my uncle leads the women through the crowd to the ship's ladder, one arm pressed to the Mistress's back. "Get aboard, you drunken louts!" he barks to the men on the quay. "And see that my wife's bags are brought to my cabin!"

Roberto and I turn back to the carriage. Again and again I glance behind me, hoping for one last sight of the people I have come to love as my family. Through the mist of tears I see a half-dozen sailors clambering up the ladder. Loud and unruly, they prod one another from behind. One is taller than the others and steadies a man in front of him. "The Master and Juan Pablo!" I whisper.

Roberto and I wait near the carriage until the quay is clear of sailors, the ladder is drawn up, and the soldiers ride away. Then we make our way through the darkness, back to the castle. It is strange sitting in the carriage alone. Without Doña Elena and Angelica beside me, I become aware of every rut and bump in the road, every creak of the carriage wheels. I weep quietly, as lost and fearful as the day I first sought help from the church and Fra Adolfo. Ah, the priest. His hatred of those who are not true Catholics seems godless to me now. I have come to believe what Juan Pablo told me, what my uncle said, too — what matters is a man's goodness, not the religious rituals he practices.

When we reach the castle stables, Leon is there. He helps me down from the carriage. "Come with me," he says, taking my hand.

I follow him, too tired and too desolate to do otherwise. He leads me to the castle kitchen. It is empty at this hour, lit only by a single torch that throws uncertain light into the shadows. He draws two chairs to the large work table, then fills a plate of leftovers from the wedding feast and cuts a square of wedding cake, which he brings to me. When he sits down, he says, "They will leave at dawn. I will not sleep until I see the ship set out to sea." Seeing me hesitate over the food, he says, "Eat, Maria. You had nothing earlier."

I am touched by his concern — both for the Delgados and for me — and reluctantly take a bite of cake. Tears are so close I can hardly speak. "I shall miss them."

"For a while." He stares hard at me. "But not always. We will return to Cáceres tomorrow. The Master told me to close up the house and deliver the keys to Señor Perreira. He hopes that things will be better someday. Then, perhaps, he will return."

"Do you think he will?"

"No. His family were once Jews. That will not be forgiven. Not during his lifetime. Perhaps not ever."

"I can never forgive myself for the part I played in hurting the family."

Leon regards me tenderly. "You have recognized your mistake and done your best to correct it. Now forgive yourself, and move on."

"How? How do I move on with the Delgados gone?"

Leon is full of ideas about what I might do, and we talk for hours. He is a practical man, as he once told me, who looks ahead, plans, then acts. He never mourns what he might have done better but simply works to change it. I like those qualities and listen to him as I would to a teacher.

I rub my eyes, trying to stay awake, and stretch my shoulders to shake off fatigue when Leon says, "Soon it will be light. Come. I will take you to the harbor so you can watch your friends depart."

He lifts me onto his horse so that I sit behind him. I lean my face against his back as we trot down the hill in the lifting dark. The horse knows its way, snorting from time to time as it tests the road. The air smells of damp earth and brine from the sea. In early light, things seem brighter, more hopeful.

Palos still sleeps, its shops closed, even the alehouse locked for the night. If soldiers are about, we are unaware of them. We dismount and walk side by side. Leon takes my hand, and this time I am not uncomfortable. I smile up at him, for it feels right and good.

The only sounds are the clop-clop of the horse's hooves and the lap of the sea on the quay. We pass two ships with torches lighting their decks. When we reach the berth where Uncle Francisco's ship lay only hours ago, it is empty. We peer out at the dark sea, where the slightest blush of morning tinges the sky. Far out, almost to the horizon, floats a dark object. I hope, I *feel* it is my uncle's ship, carrying the Delgados safely away. My heart fills with relief and joy.